Other titles by this author

HIDDEN DARKNESS

SISITERS OF DARKNESS

REALMS OF DARKNESS

BACK INTO DARKNESS

SHADOWS OF DARKNESS

DREAMS OF DARKNESS

TWISTED BLOOD.

THE ELUSIVE NEIGHBOUR

FULL MOON

YOU ARE NOT LISTENING TO ME

THE CANDLE

GRAVEYARD SHIFT

THE STRANGER

WITCHFINDER

FRIEND

KIDNAP

VENTRILOQUIST

EVIL

TALES OF HORROR AND TORMENT

KEV CARTER
Copyright
2013

ISBN   978-1-291-47921-8

THE ELUSIVE NEIGHBOUR

They had been together for several years, and had moved into this lovely house only a year ago. She was seven years his junior and sometimes she didn't like the way he spoke to her, as if she were some sort of child, even though she was twenty two years of age. She laid next to him, wondering what the future would hold. She loved him, she was sure of that, and she knew he loved her in his own way. She often laid awake at night wondering these things, thinking things over while looking at the man snoring next to her. She sighed and remembered when they use to make love all night and then again in the morning, all he seemed to do now was sleep.

It was a dark, still night, the moon was full and the window was open slightly. She heard the old van pull up outside the house and looked at her sleeping boyfriend. Knowing it a waste of time to nudge him, she got out of bed and peeped through the window down onto the road next to her house.

A tall man dressed in a old style black suit stood watching as two men carried boxes into the house next door. A large container was then slid from the back of the van, it took them some time to get it steady to lift. It was very heavy, she could see the strain in their faces as they manpowered the long box out of the van and into the house, then it was several minutes before they came back out and got into the van, driving away. The tall man stood on the street, motionless as he looked up to the night sky. She couldn't see his face at first, but he turned and looked straight up at her making her jump and pull back into the room behind the safety of her closed curtain. When she dared to peek again, sliding the material aside slightly, the man had gone.

She got back into bed and laid there listening but she could hear nothing from next door. The place had been empty for months so she was used to the quiet, and it was quiet now. She turned and snuggled into her pillow, eventually falling asleep.

The next day was Saturday, the sun was strong, the day was hot, and she was up early as usual. Her partner was still in bed, he always slept later than her at the weekends, it was something she had gotten used to.

Holding her coffee in both hands, she stared out of her kitchen window. Her garden was tidy; she liked to keep it like that, simple but nice. Glancing over the wooden fence to her neighbour's, this was not what she would call tidy, in fact she hated it, there was nothing but weeds and overgrowth. Nothing had been done to it for ages and she had, at one point, thought of jumping over the fence to weed the garden while there was no one in it, but he had said it was stupid and he would fall out with her if she did.

But now that there was someone in, she walked to her back door and unlocked it and opened the door, going into the garden. Still holding her coffee she walked to the middle of her small but well kept lawn. She tried to look as inconspicuous as possible as she glanced at the downstairs windows of the house next door, but all the curtains had been drawn. She looked up and it was the same in the upstairs rooms also.

A bit disappointed, she slowly walked back in, not knowing what exactly she wanted to see, but she knowing that she hadn't seen it. The man next door intrigued her, she didn't know the reason for this, but he did.

Finishing her coffee she walked back up to the bed room and started to get out of her night clothes to get dressed. She chose tight jeans and a loose top and, just as she had finished and was closing the wardrobe door, a voice said to her abruptly, "Can you make any more bloody noise?"

"Sorry," she said to him. Turning she saw him awake and yawning, rubbing his eyes and making that annoying noise he made every morning after he finished his yawn.

"Any chance of some breakfast?" he said scratching his head and sitting up in bed looking at her.

"What do you fancy?"

"Surprise me, I will be down for it after a shower." He slid out of bed, passed her and went into the bathroom, closing the door behind him while she stood and watched him, saying nothing. She remembered the time she used to get a kiss, get some attention, some affection. A sadness suddenly came over her as she slowly went down to the kitchen to make him his breakfast.

Later that day she was alone once again, he was out with his mate at a football match. She sat in a chair looking blankly at the window, thinking of better times and not knowing why it was no longer like that. Her daydream was broken by the phone ringing, she answered it slowly.

"Hello?" she said.

"Hello Jane? It's Tracy. How you doing, flower?" The voice came back from the receiver; she instantly smiled and sat up.

"Hi Tracy, long time no see. What are you up to?"

"Fancy going out tonight? We haven't been out for ages, just us girls. It will be just like old times, what do you say?" Her voice was full of cheer and expectancy.

"Well, I will ask Mark, but I would love to, it would be great, just like the old times."

"Why do you have to ask him?" Her voice became defensive.

"Well, to make sure he has nothing planned. Is it ok if I get back to you?"

"Well, don't leave it too long, we have a lot to catch up on, so please don't let me down."

"I will ring you back as soon as possible, Tracy, I promise."

The phone call made a smile come across her face, it had been ages since she'd gone out with one of her mates. After hanging up the phone she felt so much better, she immediately went upstairs to her wardrobe and looked for something to wear. She had not had any new clothes for months and she would love nothing more than to go into town to buy herself a new outfit for tonight, but she just couldn't afford it.

Walking over to her purse on the side table, she opened it and looked in, taking out two five pound notes and some change, then checking the little pockets in the side and looking in the main compartment again. She still found nothing more, only ten pounds and change. Her heart dropped, she knew this was not enough and doubted that Mark would give her anymore to go out with. Her heart sank, it should not be like this, he goes out whenever he wants to. She suddenly became depressed and a tear welled in her left eye, but she clenched the money in her fist and fought back the tears. She knew her friend would not mind helping her out with some drinks for a night out, but her pride would not let her do it. She wanted it to be like it used to be, to have her own money again, her own life again, her own will.

Mark came home to find her sitting in the chair looking miserable. He walked up to her and she could smell the alcohol on him before he even came close.

"What's up with you?" he asked.

"Tracy wants me to go out with her tonight for a drink but I don't have any money. It would be nice if I could go, I would like to," she looked up at him hopefully.

"I don't have any fucking money, do I? What do you think I am?" He turned and walked away towards the kitchen.

She followed him with her eyes and said nothing, but she felt the temper boil up inside her, her breathing became irregular and her palms began to sweat. She watched as he came back in and dropped onto the sofa with a sigh, stretching and looking over at her saying, "Got anything to eat in this house?"

"Could I borrow some money to go out with Tracy, please Mark?" she said it firmly and was shocked at her own bravado. Looking at him, she could see his anger rise as he looked at her with narrowed eyes.

"No, I don't have any. She is a bloody slapper, anyway, that one. I don't want you going out with her kind."

"Tracy is a good friend and she is not a slapper."

"Shag owt with a pulse she would." He reached for the remote and turned on the television.

"Will you just lend me ten pounds, please?" she raised her voice to lift over the television volume.

"Shut up and make me some food, woman. I have no money and if I did, I would not give it to you to go out with that slag." He didn't even look at her as he was talking but kept his gaze fixed on the television screen.

"Why are you so horrible to me? What have I done wrong?"

"Oh for God's sake, give it a rest, will ya. I have had a bad day, we lost two nil and it's not good, so just leave it alone." He shook his head and turned the volume up on the TV remote.

"You go out whenever you want with your mates, why can't I have a night out with mine for a change. I won't be long, just a few hours. Please, Mark?"

"For Christ sake, woman." He threw the remote control at her, missing her head by less than an inch, then he stood up and stormed over to her. She felt fear grip her and she instinctively curled away from him, lifting her hands over her head. She saw the red in his eyes, which were wide and staring as he hovered above her in a threatening manner, looking down at her pathetic position.

"No, please," she whimpered like a little puppy dog, shaking.

"Don't you ever speak to me like that again, do you hear me, never. What I do is nothing to do with you and if I want to go out, I will. I work all week and bring the money into this house and don't ever forget that." He sounded furious, she had not seen him like that before, his stare turned her to ice and she just nodded her head in agreement. He reached down and took the remote and she was relived when he walked away slowly, although he was still looking at her with hate in his eyes.

Not daring to move for several minutes, she just shook and stayed quiet. Although the incident had scared her, she had to get out of the room. Slowly and with deliberate movements, she eased off the chair and quietly moved out of the room. Listening out for any noise or movement from Mark, she went upstairs and rang her friend to say she would not be coming out, then curled up on the bed in the foetal position and wept.

Mark came up to bed later that night and said nothing to her, getting a shower and going to sleep without even acknowledging her. She laid next to him on top of the covers and looked at him sleeping next to her. She found that she could not stay there close to him, so she left the room, going to the kitchen to make herself a coffee. She was surprised to see that it was eleven thirty. Taking her cup with her, she looked out the kitchen window. The night was still and quiet, so she opened the door and welcomed the fresh, crisp night air in her lungs. Walking out the back door, she stepped into her garden where she stood there motionless, sipping her coffee and enjoying the lovely quiet time. As she stood, she felt a sudden unease come across her, a slight shiver. Turning as she was about to go back in, she suddenly jumped and dropped her coffee cup on the ground. She saw the eyes first, piercing and hypnotic, and what strange pull they had on her. He stood motionless by his closed back door, dressed in the same old style black suit she had seen him a few nights before. He was watching her with an expressionless face, a face that had been lived in, a face she would never forget. Thin but strong features, a handsome but disturbing gaze, he smiled and slightly bowed his head in an apologetic manner. When he lifted his head once again he had a friendly smile on his face. "I'm so sorry if I startled you." His voice was strong but kind and without accent.

"It's ok," she said, smiling as she bent down to pick up her broken coffee cup.

"I like to watch the night sky myself, it is an escape for me."

"An escape?" She stood and walked closer to him and to his back door.

"Yes, the night is a special time for special people." He stood motionless and looked her straight in the eye, although not in a threatening way.

"I don't know about that, but I do like the quiet and the peace"

"The peace and quiet of centuries can be felt in the night air if you have the feel for it, you just need the heart and desire to feel it."

"Have you moved in alright and everything?"

"Yes, thank you. I will not be here for very long, I have to return to my home."

"Home? And where is that, may I ask?"

"A long way from here." He turned his stare from her and looked up into the night, taking a long breath of air and slowly releasing it from his lungs.

"So you just rent this house then?"

"Yes, just for a short while."

"Oh, I see." She looked away from him and down her garden for no reason, edging closer to her back door.

"Please forgive my manners. My name is Kovac, Peter Kovac."

"Jane."

"I'm sorry if I make you nervous. I do assure you, it is unintentional. " He smiled a warm smile which she returned.

"That's okay, you just have to be careful these days."

"Yes, you do, you have no idea who you are talking to a lot of the time, and if you did, you would be shocked I'm sure. But I do mean you no harm, Jane."

"Well it's been nice meeting you, Mister Kovac, I hope you, err, well I have to go now, goodnight." She smiled and went into her back door and locked it.

He stood smiling and said nothing. He didn't move for some time, but when she looked again out of her window, he had gone.

She took a deep breath and went into the front room, where she sat down and eventually fell into an uneasy sleep on the settee.

She was awakened by Mark coming down the stairs and making himself a coffee in the kitchen. She stood and stretched her aching muscles, she did not sleep well at all. Mark came over and stood in front of her, saying in a uncomforting and unconvincing voice, "Sorry, but you pissed me off."

"I only wanted a few drinks with Tracy, that's all."

"Yeah, well, it's over now." He sat down and switched on the television and, as far as he was concerned, that was the end of it.

She looked at him expressionlessly for a few moments then went up for a shower, the water refreshed her and she felt much more awake and alive after it, then she got dressed and came downstairs. After making some breakfast for them both, the rest of the morning was spent sitting in silence, watching the television. Mark went out after dinner, to his friends he said, but she knew he was going to the pub. She sat once again, alone and sad on the chair. The television was on but she was not listening to it, until a news item came on about a local farm.

This got her attention, she listened to the story about several cows that had been attacked and killed, ripped to pieces. The daughter of the farmer said she had seen a man in black running away as they went out to investigate the noise of the cows and the dogs barking. She didn't see his face, just saw that he was in a black suit and running away from the field.

She stood up and went to the kitchen, looking out to where she was talking to her neighbour the night before. The sun was shining and it all looked different now in daylight. She opened the door and went out, looking up at the house next door where she once again saw it was all in darkness, curtains drawn, looking cold and empty. The phone rang and she went back in, locking the door behind her. She answered the phone coldly, but smiled when she realized that it was her friend Tracy who asked in a concerned tone, "Are you okay, Jane?"

"Yes I'm fine, Tracy. Thanks."

"Sorry you could not make it last night, I thought the bastard wouldn't let you out"

"I will try and get out next time, okay?"

"Well don't worry about it, but you have to get away from him, Jane."

"We're just going through a bad time, that's all. Hey, have you heard the news about those cows being ripped apart at the farm?" she asked eagerly, trying and hoping to change the subject.

"Yes, it was on the news this morning. Bloody kids probably, drugged up. They want locking up and fed on bread and water for six month, the bloody lot of them."

"They say a man was seen running away in a black suit."

"Probably some bloody tramp or something."

"Do you think?"

"Yeah, it's obvious, they kip down on farms don't they, and he saw the little bastards and fled before they did the same to him no doubt."

"It's horrible, isn't it? They say it looked like they had been ripped apart."

"You sound scared, Jane, do you think it was a werewolf or something?" She started to laugh out loud over the phone.

"No I don't, you silly sod, but it is horrible."

"Yes, and it wasn't a full moon last night either, was it?"

"I'm serious Tracy. Listen, there is a man who has moved in next door, he is weird, he was out in his back garden last night very late, and he was wearing a black suit, and all the curtains are drawn during the day"

"What?"

"Yes, and there is never any sound from next door, he's only been there a few days."

"Bloody hell, he doesn't speak with a Transylvanian accent, does he?" She started to laugh again.

"I'm bloody serious, Tracy."

"Oh right, I've got it. He went out last night and fed on cows because he fancied a stake. Get it, a stake?"

"Oh shut up, you silly sod."

Tracy was laughing uncontrollably on the phone and took a few minutes to calm down so she could speak again. "Oh, come on, Jane, you always have had an overactive imagination. So Dracula next door went and fed on cows last night. Ripped them apart so no one would see the fang marks, bet that is what you're thinking, isn't it? Tell me, why cows then? Why not young virgins in distress? Mind you, you're right, he won't find any virgins round here," she started to laugh again.

"Tracy, your being silly, now stop it. I wish I had not told you."

"I'm sorry, flower, but you should hear yourself, you sound scared to death."

"Think I'm being silly?"

"Yes, just a bit. Why don't we meet up one day next week when your toss pot of a boyfriend out at work?"

"Yes, that would be great" Jane smiled at the thought.

"Good. I will ring you tomorrow then and we will arrange it. I will get a day off work and we shall have a girls day out, and don't bloody worry about money either."

"Okay, Tracy, thanks. You're a good friend."

"Well, you know I can't help it," she said jokingly. "That's what friends are for, silly."

Jane was in a good mood again, the incident the night before with Mark suddenly didn't seen as important, she was lifted and felt much better now that she had something to look forward to. A day out with her friend was going to be wonderful, just what she needed and wanted.

She awoke with a sudden jolt, but didn't know why, Mark was snoring next to her she looked at the clock; it was one o'clock in the morning. She slid out of bed and went downstairs as if she were sleepwalking, then she walked to her back door and opened it, wandering out into the darkness in her night dress. She was awake but felt half asleep, it was a funny but nice feeling.

"Good evening, Jane."

She turned with a start and looked right into the eyes of her elusive neighbour. He was standing in the same position as the last time, motionless and staring into her eyes. She felt no fear, no unrest, no suspicion and she didn't understand why.

"Good evening," she said to him, walking closer to him until they were facing each other across the fence, so close that they could touch.

"I know you are sad, Jane. I can feel sadness, I can see it and I can help you, if you wish it. And I think you do wish it, Jane, don't you?"

"Yes," she said with a nod. His eyes were burning into her soul; she had never felt like this before, never felt this intensity with another human being, with anything before. It was a warm glow that was drawing her to him from within.

"I am leaving this evening, Jane, and will never return to this place, but I would like to leave you with some thing before I go. Something to make you happy again, to make you alive again"

"Yes," is all she could say--all she wanted to say.

He came closer to her and she could feel his breath on her face, their eyes still locked in an eternal stare, a deep look of endless depth. His lips came close to hers and he gently kissed her, she responded with an identical kiss, his lips were cold, but his presence was warm and inviting.

He moved from her lips and slid down to her neck, again kissing and biting very slightly. She moaned and his hands took her and, with tremendous strength but without hurting her in the slightest, he lifted her up and over the fence with a superhuman strength no man should have. He put her down in front of him and put his arms round her, kissing her again. She felt so safe, so right, so comfortable in his embrace. He moved down her body, kissing gently as he did.

Crouching down, he lifted her night dress up and stroked her leg and inner thigh as she again moaned with the feel of his touch. He kissed her legs then positioned himself between them. She let one leg fall outwards as she stood and waited for the bite that she knew was going to come. High up on her left inner thigh, out of sight but just as effective, his teeth were long and thrust into her skin, puncturing and plunging deep into her vein.

He drank slowly and almost lovingly, tasting her life liquid with deep sucks and long indulgence of her blood. She winced at the initial break of her skin, but any pain soon passed and she felt all her life's worries and hurts were being drained from her and being replaced with an energy she had never known. He stopped and pulled away from her but she didn't want him to stop and she put her fingers in his hair as he stood back up.

Pulling him close to her, she passionately kissed his blood stained mouth, tasting her own blood, tasting what he had tasted. It was better than any sex she had ever had, more orgasmic and more satisfying than any feeling she had ever experienced in her life; she didn't want it to ever stop, didn't want to be away from this man ever again. She wanted to be his, would do anything for him for the rest of her life. The sensation in her body was amazing; she could feel the blood rushing through her veins, her heart beating faster, stronger, like never before. She felt like she could do anything.

He pulled away from her and looked deep into her eyes, she could hear his voice but could not see his lips moving. "You can do anything you want to do, Jane, anything. Don't let anyone stop you or get in your way, be yourself and never let anyone stop you from doing so. You have an eternity on this earth, Jane. In darkness, roam and do as you wish but feed wisely and only take human blood when you have to, the blood of animals do not arouse so much suspicion. Take care, Jane, goodbye, and enjoy your eternal life."

He slid away from her, but she didn't see where he went. She breathed heavily and looked up into the sky, a strong feeling in her belly made her take a big lungful of air. Her heart was racing, her veins were pumping blood fast round her body, her adrenalin was high and she felt like she could do anything.

She didn't sleep that night, just laid in bed with a feeling of such elation. She fell asleep during the day and awoke when Mark came home at about six o'clock. She didn't care, she was content and laid on top of the bed. She heard him come up the stairs, and storm into the room. "What the fuck is all this? I'm out working all day and you are in bloody bed? Where is my tea?" he screamed at her.

She calmly got up from the bed and faced him, there was no fear at all in her eyes or face, and she smiled and softly said, "Do you mind if I feed first?"

"What?" is all Mark said, his last word.

She tore into him with a ferocious strength that shocked him into silence and ripped his throat from his neck with a precise tear-he was quietened for good. She fed on him and drank deeply, relishing her first kill, but knowing this would not be her last. Throwing the carcass on the bed, she went and had a shower then calmly got dressed.

It was the first night of the rest of her undead life.

FULL MOON

The moon will be up soon, it will be full and I will be changing, I like it, Although others may think it a curse, Some are tormented and haunted by it, but I like it. The pain can be enjoyable if you know how to control it. The savage lust and need for feeding comes with its own benefits. The moon will be up soon, high in the sky and I will howl to it and be off for the night. I might feed or I might just run and kill for the sake of it. It all depends on how the hunger takes hold of me. I have a degree of control and I know what I am doing at all times, but can not or just do not want to stop. The trick is to make it look like an accident or make it look like something else has done what you have done.

No one can ever know what I am, or what I become on a full moon. No one will ever truly understand it unless they are going through it themselves, how could they? I leave a terrible mess of the bodies sometimes, ripped apart and torn to pieces, But, I do not have any remorse about it, I feel nothing for them. for I do not know them. I am clever and always find ways of covering my tracks, and disguising what has really happened. I do not have relationships and always remain a loner. It suits me and I am a lot happier with it. Over the years I have developed the best answer for my situation. And other people are not in the equation. The moon will be full and rising high in the night sky soon, I can feel it in my blood, a stirring in my very soul. The excitement and rush of power that races through me, the energy and force that is unstoppable. I run faster and jump higher, I have adrenaline rushing through me and my strength is incredible. Oh yes, I like it, I do not see it as a curse at all I see it more of a gift, a chance to become stronger and faster and power charged like never before.

No one is faster or stronger or more powerful than me, I know of a few others like me, but they try to repress it, to stop the power, I know of one who locks himself away every full moon and is left in his own torment in his own cell. It is a horrible thing to do, to cage a beast and not let it run free, but he does this and he pays for this with his own suffering. I like it and let it run free, I enjoy it and will always enjoy it, I am grateful and happy I have this amazing gift to change, to shape shift into a beautiful and powerful creature every full moon. It is a secret only I know and only I will ever know, I was scared the first time but soon came to understand the capability and power of what I become. The first attack and the bite that made me what I am, was very bad, I must admit and I had no idea what had bit me, but I soon found out the next full beautiful moon. I have never wanted to change back I have never regretted being bit, all those years ago. I have no idea who changed me, but they didn't kill me, They made me strong and powerful and so very special. I am grateful.

The heat is boiling my blood now, the moon is doing its magic on me. I feel the rush going through my heart and body. My teeth are aching my bones are aching. It is going to happen soon, the change, the transformation, the wonderful feeling of becoming something so much better than I am now. The change from a weak feeble man, into a strong and powerful beast, ferocious and vigorous and savage

The moon is rising I can see it, I am going to get ready and be gone into the night, I wonder who I will meet and if I will feed or if I will just rip apart, be careful tonight, it might just be you. You will not see me but I will see you and smell you long before I get near. And when I spot you? Well, you will have to wait and see won't you….?

21

22

YOU ARE NOT LISTENING TO ME

"But you don't know anything about him," Diane said to her young friend.

"He is gorgeous and we have chatted lots of times on the internet."

"But you still do not know anything about him. Let me come with you. I won't get in your way and it will be much safer and, if he is genuine, then he won't mind."

"Oh, stop pestering. It is only a little fishing trip on his boat and he's just taking me down the river. What's up, are you jealous?" Tracy said in a slightly bitchy tone to her older friend.

"Not at all and because you are young and immature I will disregard that last remark. But you're thinking with your vagina and not your head, girl!"

"Oh, that is gross. What a silly thing to say." She shook her head and pulled a screwed up face at her friend sitting across the table from her in the coffee shop.

"It is dangerous meeting people you do not know, especially these days. Tell me where you are going and let me drop you off so I can look at him, then I will come and pick you back up again. How is that?"

"I am meeting Geoff and we are having a little fishing down the river in his boat and then we are coming back and that is all!"

"You have never fished in your life, what do you know about fishing? And once you're on that boat in the middle of nowhere, you're stuck. You will not be able to run away, will you?"

"I don't want to run away, he is dead fit." She giggled like a little schoolgirl while taking a sip from her half empty coffee cup.

"Just be careful. Please take your phone and ring me, okay? You can at least do that, can't you?" Diane pleaded rather than asked.

"Yes, I will do that if it will shut you up. You sound like my bloody mother sometimes. I am seventeen and I can take care of myself."

***

The boat was a light craft, not very big, and it was painted red and white. Geoff was coming in from a fishing trip; he had been out since the early hours. It was not unusual for him to leave so early and he was a regular figure around the boat yard.

He pulled his craft up to the edge and tied it off securely. He jumped off and walked up the small hill, waving and nodding hello to a few people who knew him as he went. He looked at his watch and quickened his step heading up to the car park and his car. He just had time to get home and get a shower before he had to pick up Diane.

***

The day was nice, not too warm, but Diane still wore her skirt above the knee. She had worn her push-up bra on and a tight blouse. She showed her young, firm body off very well, but was naive about the stares that she received. Tracy had told her on many occasion to stop flaunting, it can be dangerous, but she liked the attention and she did it whenever she could.

Taking her phone out, she sent Tracy a message saying that she was well and all was good. Then she turned her phone off and put it in the little bag that she was carrying. She walked the short distance from the bus stop to the river where she had arranged to meet Geoff.

She misses a breath as her nerves take her by surprise when she see's him resting up against a wall. He is looking out across the river and does not see her right away, giving her a little time to look him up and down. Gorgeous is how she would describe him and she had always thought so from the first time she saw the picture of himself that he had emailed to her from the pen pal site they both had joined.

He turned and looked at her as she walked down the road. She smiled and saw that his face was a little bit older than the photo he had sent her, but she disregarded the thought as the excitement coursed through her veins.

"Diane, I'm so glad you could make it!" His voice was friendly and his smile welcoming and reassuring to her.

She smiled back and said a little nervously, "So glad you could make it too."

She was standing in front of him and didn't know what to do, so she just smiled and let her immaturity and inexperience show through.

He smiled back at her and made her feel a little more comfortable.

"Well, let's get this first awkward moment over with, then we can relax and get to know each other a little better." He leaned forward and give her a little friendly kiss on the cheek, surprising her, then he smiled and pointed to his car, starting to walk the few yards towards it.

Her face showed her confusion as she looked around. She could see that there was no one about and she felt a little vulnerable.

"Where is your boat? I thought we were going fishing on the river?" she asked.

"We are. You're not listening to me. My boat is in the boat yard; we have to go get it first, silly. Come on."

He grinned at her as he opened the door for her and waited.

She nervously smiled back as she slowly walked to the car and got in. Feeling around in her bag unobtrusively, she made sure she had her phone close at hand and now wished that she had not turned it off.

He closed the door, then hurried around and got in the other side. He started the car and was away very quickly. He drove down the hill and out onto the main road.

Once they were on their way, he settled back in his seat, glancing over at her and saying, "You look absolutely gorgeous, Diane. Stunning, in fact"

His smile again comforted her and she relaxed a little, saying, "Thank you. You're not too bad yourself. How old are you? I thought you said you were nineteen?" She noticed his face close up and could tell he was much older.

"What is age? It is only a number. It is how old you feel that counts. I bet you feel much older than you are, don't you? I just bet you are mature enough to be twenty-five and you are sick of people telling you different, treating you like a child. Am I right?"

"Yes, you are. I am mature and I can take care of myself," she said with new found confidence, nodding her head once to reinforce the fact.

"There you go then. What is age? It is just a number. We are as old as we want to be, right?" He glanced at her and smiled broadly.

She melted at his blue eyes and friendly smile and could not help but smile back at him.

"So where is your boat?"

"Not far, just down in the boat yard. It will take us about ten minutes to get there, that's all."

"Okay. How many other girls do you take out on your boat then?" She smiled and tried to relax, but asking the question made her nervous at the answer she might get.

"Oh, Diane, you're not listening to me. I don't have a string of girlfriends, I told you that when we chatted online. My last girlfriend never listened to me or understood me, but you live and learn, don't you?"

"Yes, you do. Well, I think your last girlfriend was mad to let you go."

Geoff looked at her for a moment then smiled at her, saying, "Thank you for your kind words. She just sank out of sight in the end."

"Her loss, my gain. I think you're gorgeous, Geoff."

"Thank you, Diane. I think you're gorgeous too. Maybe after we have caught some fish you would like a drink?"

"Oh, yes, I would like that." She settled back in her seat much more at ease and sighed a sigh of contentment.

"Good, so would I."

It took them about fifteen minutes to reach the boat yard. He pulled the car up around the back of the large shed. He stopped and looked around the place as if searching for something.

"Is this it then?" Diane asked, looking a little puzzled at his strange actions.

"Yes. Just wait here and I will go and sort out the paperwork, then we can be gone." Before she could ask what he meant, he sheepishly got out of the car and disappeared around the back of the large shed in front of them.

Diane searched in her bag and took her phone out. She turned it on and waited for it to start. It seemed to take so long. She kept glancing up to where Geoff had gone, then eagerly back to her phone. She shook it slightly, impatient for it to start. First she got the light on then the battery meter, but no signal. She cursed and held it up, trying to get a signal on the damn thing, but she could not. She threw it back into her bag and sighed, then jolted in fear as someone banged on the window and opened the door violently.

"Come on, then," Geoff said, smiling at her startled look.

"You idiot, you scared me!" she said, slowly getting out of the car.

He hurried her along, saying nothing. She was too busy trying to look around and find out where she was to notice how uncomfortable he was in getting her to the boat. They stepped onto the craft and she turned, seeing nobody about. The place seemed to be deserted.

Geoff put on a long jacket that covered him completely. "Okay, here we go," he said, untying the boat and going to the small wheel house to start her up.

She walked a little unsteadily to the front and joined him in the small, dirty wooden enclosure. She began to regret this straight away as she noticed the state of the boat; it was not what she expected at all.

"Where is everyone? The place looks deserted."

"We will just sail out a little to the river, then we will cast off and catch ourselves some fish." His mood changed as he started up the engine and eased the vessel out of the boat yard and up the river. He eased the speed and they went along at a nice steady pace.

She held onto the wooden side of the cabin so she didn't fall over. It was not a smooth ride at all, but as they slowed down and hit calmness in the water on the river it was much more enjoyable. Looking around the dirty boat, she saw two fishing rods and three large concrete blocks.

"What are those blocks for?" she asked him curiously

"Stability, silly. You're not listening again." He pulled the boat to the middle of the river and carried on away.

It was getting wider and deeper and Diane was regretting her decision more and more. She reached into her bag and looked at her phone. Noticing that she had a signal here brought a little smile to her face.

"Okay, let's get sorted then, shall we?"

He stopped the boat and came out of the cabin. He looked around again and then smiled at Diane, who gave him a false smile back. He took two folding chairs and opened them up for the both of them to sit on and then made ready the fishing rods.

He cast one into the river and gave this to her, gesturing for her to sit down, which she did. He then cast out the other rod and sat next to her.

Diane held the rod awkwardly and looked around at the banking of the river some distance away. She was not the best of swimmers, but thought she could make it if she needed to.

"Isn't this nice and peaceful?" he asked, looking at her straight in the eye.

She nodded and gave a little weak smile. She definitely did not enjoy sitting in a dirty boat while holding a rod into some water.

"Yes, it's quiet. Do you come here a lot then?" she asked nervously. She had noticed he had stopped smiling and he looked blank and different somehow.

"I come here when I want to remember and sometimes forget."

"I don't understand, remember and forget?"

"Yes. Remember that it was inevitable and forget what others might think."

"You are not making sense to me, Geoff." She was becoming even more nervous and sighed out loud.

"Why are you sighing? Are you not having fun? Isn't this what you wanted? You said to me when we messaged that you would like to go fishing with me. Well, here you are fishing with me and your bloody sighing." His voice was cold and mean.

She began to shake and didn't know what to say. She didn't have the experience or the maturity or the confidence to match him.

Just at that moment, her line became tight, nearly pulling her rod from her hand. She gripped and pulled up with all her might, taking her thoughts and concentration away from the man next to her.

He glanced over and put his rod down. He smiled again, that melting smile, and helped her pull the rod up. It was bending in an incredible arch and she could not pull it anymore, she just did not have the strength to do so.

Finally the rod snapped violently, making her scream and jump back. She let go and sat back down in the chair. She was back up again quickly to look over the side at her catch. She gasped and put her hand over her mouth as she saw the mangled face of a dead woman, wide-eyed and staring up at her from the water, wrapped in fishing line and looked hideous. Crying and shaking, Diane sat back down into the chair, petrified.

Geoff was unmoved and just pushed the body back down with the rod, watching it sink slowly down to the bottom again. He turned and looked at the quivering, pathetic sight in front of him and his face dropped. He shook his head and stared at her.

Diane, her hands shaking, reached into her bag and pulled out her phone. It was knocked from her hand and kicked away from her.

He stood above her and looked down through eyes that were cold and calculating.

"She didn't understand me. She kept going on and on, just like the rest. Didn't listen to me, just like you. Well, you might as well join them."

"Geoff, please," she whimpered.

"Geoff? Who is that? I am not called Geoff. Don't worry, I will tie three blocks to you so you won't come back to bother anyone like she did. She always has to stick her nose in, doesn't she? She had to come up to have a look at you." He clenched his fist and stamped his foot in anger.

Without warning, he took the rod he had been fishing with and whacked her across the head with it. She fell off the chair as the sharp pain hit her face and, before she could stagger back up, the fishing line was wrapped around her face and neck and pulled tight. It cut deep and blood smeared her face and neck as she struggled and tried in vain to get free. The line was wrapped around and around her neck and pulled tighter until she could not breathe and her life was gone.

He threw the dead body to the side and stood up. Taking a deep breath, he looked around the river and along the empty banking. He turned and took some rope from a box and began to tie the concrete blocks to the body of Diane.

He threw the phone he had knocked out of her hand into the river and then looked at the lifeless body, saying, "What was that? Oh, no, the water won't be cold. The others will keep you warm. I will tie three blocks to you so you won't be able to come back. It is good that you are listening to me now, so much better, don't you think?"

He then lifted the body and blocks and rolled them off the boat into the river, watching impassively as they sank down out of sight. Whistling, he put the chairs away and took off the waterproof jacket he had put on. It was covered with blood, so he dropped it into the water and, with his other hand, rubbed the blood off it to some degree. He then casually shook it and hung it back up in the cabin.

Taking a small hose pipe, he hosed the deck off and the blood splashed away through little holes in the side. When he was satisfied he had done his job well, he started the boat back up and headed up the river to his house.

And straight to his computer, where he was chatting to a nice girl he had met on line.

THE CANDLE

The candle burned steady, it flickered every now and then, but it showed there was no draft what so ever around it, the door was locked, the windows shut, curtains drawn, it lit the room very dimly. The wax had dripped down the candle on one side, where it had broken out of the small reservoir that had been made by the wick burning down.

The red wax had made a pool on the old wooden table where it was stood. Where it has been stood for some time, gently burning away and slowly killing its self as its life blood, the wax, was melted and flowed away onto the table.

It was the only light emanating in the small room, the only form of illumination that was available to see what had happened. The Candle had witnessed it all, the argument, the torture, the killing, but it never faltered in its duty, still it stayed lit, and it just burned away there on the table.

It had all happened some hours before, that is when it was lit, then placed on the table, the man and women then started to argue. She did not want to stay in the room. He was insisting she did, and pulled her by the hair throwing her to the ground. She fell with a sickening thud that shocked her system.

He had then began to shout abuse at her, threatening her and spitting down at her on the floor. She tried to stand and was violently knocked back down again. Trying to fight him she lashed out but was hit and slapped hard. She was over- weight and this seemed to be what the argument was about. He was shouting abuse at her about her over size and obesity. The argument grew loud and violent. She was crying and desperately trying to stand, she found it very hard with her size, he easily pushed her back down and kept her there. He then kicked her hard in the side. She curled up in pain rolling away from him. He followed and kicked her again, calling her fat and vile, and other derogatory names. Her tears were lost on him, he just continued kicking her as she grew weaker and less able to defend herself.

He was out of breath when he had done, she was sobbing and curled up like a defenseless baby. He stood over her and shouted abuse down to her. But she was not listening, her head was thumping from inside where he had kicked it, her side screamed out every time she tried to move, and the retched pain in her insides when she tried to breathe, too heavy.

He looked down at her with a disgusted look on his face, he was shaking and trying to catch his breath.

There was silence for a moment, the candle flickered doing its job and just lighting enough of the dark room to make a difference. The flame going straight up and burning the wick nicely.

The sobs of torment could be heard from the floor, the face of the man looked positively evil as he stared down at her, with hate, disgust and anger in his eyes.

He looked round the room, then left by the door, locking it from outside and was gone. She still could not move, the vicious and injurious attack had done some serious damage. She could not breath without the pain tearing through her whole body, her head was like a thumping jack hammer, her breathing became desperate and irregular. The fear with in her made it all worse and she began to panic, causing her breathing to become more painful and difficult. All she could do was stay perfectly still, any movement hurt and caused her sickening pain. Trying to calm herself she stayed quiet and still.

The candle had burned down at least half an inch before the door was opened again, the strong smell of beer could be smelt as the man staggered in, the draft from the doorway made the candle flicker and the flame move from side to side. The door was slammed shut and the man stood there swaying. He walked over to the woman on the floor and dropped to his knees, she shied away from him in fear as he tried to reach out to her. He became angry and pushed her away from him grunting as he did. She cried out in pained anguish, this angered the man once again and he began to shout obscenities at her, saying she was fat, overweight, ruined his life, lazy.

His final brutal assault was ferocious and nasty, he hit her, punched her and kicked her, she was quiet and still half way through his barrage of feet and fists, But he kept going with his onslaught of violence. When he had done he dropped to the floor exhausted. He eventually staggered out of the room several minutes later.

It had been still and quiet ever since. The candle still burned but was now very small and would not be lasting much longer. It flickered and faltered as it got smaller and would soon extinguish its self. The room would be in darkness then and what happens the candle would not be part of, but in its short life it had served its purpose well. It had not gone out and had burned constantly lighting the small room so the people could see what they were doing and what was happening. It had now come to the end of its life, flickering for a few last times it died and was gone.

The End

GRAVEYARD SHIFT

The memorial graveyard was dark, cold, desolate and lonely. Crows were squawking high up, unseen in the tree tops around the perimeter of the walled resting place for the dead.

It was summer and it was past midnight. Since the crows always made themselves known, day or night, not many people took notice. It was not in town and there were no houses nearby.

The war heroes were laid here; the men who had fought for their country and gave the ultimate sacrifice. The men who had died fighting, leaving loved ones at home wondering and worrying. Not knowing the horror that their sons, husbands, and fathers were enduring all those miles away in other countries, other lands, other worlds.

The large stone tower stood in a place of pride in the centre, engraved upon it the names of the men from the area who were missing or were killed in the Great War.

People now seemed to take the place for granted. Few people bothered to read it. Few people came and sat on the bench next to it to look, remember and give thanks. The ones who had are now gone, having been old men and women who knew the dead and missing or knew what they went through because they gone through it too. The only difference was that they had come home to tell the tale.

No, no one had the respect now. It was disgusting the way the young never want to know how they can live their free lives, in a free society, in a free country. They don't bother to even think of the sacrifice that has been made for them by others. It never occurs to them to be grateful to those who gave their lives so that they could live in such a free world.

On this day, Thursday, an afternoon school trip was going to visit the memorial and be told about some of the men whose names were on it.

Their teacher, Mister Topham, had reason for this. His father had helped to build the memorial tower and it was the anniversary of his death. He did not tell his students this, but he saw it as a fitting tribute to him.

The school mini bus stopped outside the two large, black, rusting iron gates and the class climbed down. Mister Topham, a thin man with black-rimmed glasses on looked over his flock from the step of the bus. He counted them on at school and now was counting them off again, all twelve of them.

"Right listen to me," he said with authority. "No one go wondering off, we stick as a unit. Is that clear?"

He got a nod and a few genuine grunts for replies and nodded briskly himself. He locked the bus and led the way into the graveyard.

The crows were busy cawing and cackling, causing some of the students to look up into the tree tops. They soon gave up when nothing could be seen of them. The noise was there but catching sight was another matter it seemed.

Topham's flock comprised of boys and girls all aged about fifteen years. None of them wanted to be there, they simply saw it as an afternoon away from class. Some fresh air away from the boring school and boring education they were acquiring.

Topham walked to the memorial tower proudly. His father had helped to put this here and here he was all these years later, standing on its step. He looked up and waited for the attention of his students.

"Okay, listen. I'm going to tell you a little about some of the men whose names are here on the fine stone work of this beautiful memorial."

He rose to full height before he began and took a deep breath. He had rehearsed this and wanted to get it right.

Looking very bored and disinterested, Ray scanned the area as his teacher was telling the class about the sacrifice made for him and people like him.

He noticed black wings flying past and settling in the trees, but lost sight of it. He turned and looked at Gail, who was standing in front of him. Her tight skirt showed off her nice tight arse, he thought, and it brought a smile to his face. He sighed and looked back to his teacher whose voice was louder, he was in full swing.

"And Private Cooper, he was shot in the eye but miraculously still managed to save his friends life…"

Topham was in full teaching mode telling how Cooper died, but Ray was not interested. He looked at all the girl's backsides and compared them, coming to the conclusion Gail's was the best.

Putting his hands down deep in his pockets, he looked at Topham and again opened his ears to the torture.

"Mathews was a very brave man. He lived not far from here, on the common. He was under attack with his unit when he was shot twice in the leg and, in spite of it, he gave covering fire as his comrades got to safety. Later he was retrieved and taken to the hospital. The leg amputated but, despite his bravery, he died the next day."

The girls in the group found it all a bit disturbing and were showing their disgust by turning to each other with frowning faces and shaking heads.

"The last two men I want to talk about are Larry Wilson and Peter Summers.

Larry was a huge man, over six feet tall and built like a tank. Peter only a small man but the heart of a lion…"

By now the class was not listening to their teacher, he was showing great interest and enthusiasm but they wanted more interesting things, exciting things, more modern things, not old war stories.

Ray stepped close behind Gail and pressed himself against her, feeling her firm, warm rear end on his crotch. She didn't move but said quietly, "Move it or lose it, Ray."

"Lose it where?" he teased.

"You wouldn't want to know," she told him flatly.

"Are you sure of that?" he said with a grin.

"Are you listening back there?" Topham shouted at Ray.

"Yes, Sir," said Ray. "A soldier with one eye, another with one leg, a big one and a small one, what a fighting force, eh sir?"

The class laughed at his insolence and it relieved the boredom. He smiled, loving the attention.

"Come here, lad," Topham ordered in a restrained voice.

Ray walked cockily through the class enjoying his centre stage. He smirked as he came up to his teacher, who didn't look impressed.

"Sir?" he said, his head tilted to one side in a cocky manner.

Topham looked at him then the class. He was serious and the class could see he was annoyed. He spoke loudly but without shouting.

"Okay class, seeing you are not taking me seriously and because Ray here is trying to be the big man, we are going back early and all of you will have to give me, by

Monday morning, a four thousand word essay on this memorial, the men on it and the history behind it. This can be found in the library and on the school computer."

"Oh, Sir," the chorus rang out. They were suddenly awake and annoyed; it was not a popular request.

"I was going to make an afternoon of it for you and also make it easy. By your lack of enthusiasm and lack of interest, disrespect, total childishness, and of course Ray's sarcasm, it's up to you." He was poker-faced and not going to move.

He was annoyed and perturbed, seeing it as a hit against him, his father and the men on the memorial. He had been proud of the men who gave their lives for their country. Proud men who wanted and deserved to be remembered. His father was there and told his son all about it, he wanted to share this with his class but he had not got any response. Just like he had not got any back at the school. He had arranged this bus in his own time and could see now it was a waste of time.

Ray was now suddenly not popular anymore, he was scowled at and swore at by his classmates who saw him as the reason their weekend was going to be spent writing and reading, instead of laughing and playing.

Ray tried to act the big hero but no one was impressed. Gail refused to talk to him when he winked at her on the bus, his friends shook their heads and he was snubbed all the way back to school. He sat alone on the bus looking out of the window and he turned and looked at Topham every now and again with a horrid, hateful look on his face.

Topham did not speak on the way back. He took them back to school and they collected their books and spent the rest of the day in the school library.

Ray logged onto the internet and typed in the memorial name. What he saw made him rage; he suddenly knew why Topham had acted so madly.

The information he saw was the men who built the tower; it was a picture from a local newspaper of the time with the names of the men who erected it. He looked at the name Topham then he looked at the photo. A thin man and even with similar glasses. The resemblance was unmistakable.

He hated Topham at this time and would never forgive him for causing him to be outcast by his friends for a while. Gail wasn't talking to him and he felt mad and angry at his teacher. Who did this Topham think he was, causing him all this upset. He looked at the photo and knew what he was going to do.

The rest of the class were busy researching, but he had no intention of handing in any essay. He had better things to be doing at the weekend, better things to be planning and his revenge was going to be sweet. He would laugh about it for a long time to come. Pity he couldn't tell any of his friends. He didn't trust any of them at this time and so knew he must do it alone.

He idled away the rest of the day watching the pathetic pupils all writing about a piece of stone Topham was so passionate about. He shook his head and just waited. His time was to come and Topham's face would be a picture when he found out. The thought of it made him smile and kept him going through the afternoon.

He waited and said nothing of his plan. It was his and his alone. No one was going to know, no one would be able to prove a thing, but he would know and he wanted to see Topham's face when he found out.

He could not stop smiling to himself as he sat in a chair and leaned back. He knew all his friends would come back to his side soon, he would be the man again.

After school, Ray went back to the memorial and sat on the bench looking at the stone creation. He loathed it. Topham had all this respect for it and it's only a piece of ugly stone with some names engraved in it. How sad is Topham to have such a passion for something so stupid, he thought.

He looked up when he heard the crows squawking above. He hated them as well, bloody noisy things he thought. It was quiet and still except for the birds making their irritating noise. He couldn't see them, could just hear them.

Picking some small stones up from the ground, he threw them one by one at the memorial, watching them bounce off and away. He then stood and walked out of the place, going home and leaving the place empty, deserted and cold.

Saturday night was usually full of mischievous fun for him, but this Saturday night was different. He was not out with his friends, he was out alone. He told no one what he was going to do, told no one what was in the black bag he was taking out.

He sneaked out of his house and went the old way through the woods to where he was going. There was less chance of him being seen this way around. He had waited until it was almost dark; the moon was out full and the night was still and calm.

Walking through the woods he came to a road, crossed this with a run and then was again unseen in the shrubbery by the side. It took him about forty-five minutes to reach the outskirts of the town where he caught sight of the memorial.

It looked gothic, like something out of a horror movie. The walled perimeter holding it in, holding it in the past, holding in the memory of the dead. Ray looked at it from a distance and thought how out of place the whole graveyard looked.

He could see no one there, nothing moving. The only light he could see by was a full moon which, strangely, lit the memorial and the internal area, but outside of the walls it seemed noticeably darker.

He thought this odd at first but dismissed it as he heard the crows, the ever present crows. Even at this distance he could not get away from them.

He headed down toward them and the stone memorial Topham had so much affection for, the bag swinging by his side. He reached the outer wall with a thud and rested against it for a moment. Walking around to the gates, he went in.

The place was lit by the moon and he could clearly see what he was doing then he looked back out of the gate and noticed the difference in darkness. With a confused look on his face, he shrugged his shoulders then turned and went up to the memorial.

Putting his bag down, he took out a can of red spray paint, a hammer and chisel and a tin of yellow gloss that he had stolen from his father's shed.

"Okay, Topham, we will see what damage we can do to your bloody shit piece of crap stone, shall we?" He took the can and shook it so the small ball bearing inside rattled, frantically agitating the paint. He looked around and then started to write a large W on the ground, suddenly stopping and looking up.

The noise was gone. The noise of the crows was gone and it was now deadly silent. He carried on and wrote an A followed by N then K E R S.

The red paint looked horrid on the stone ground in front of the memorial. Standing there in the moonlight like some large lost symbol of a past civilisation, it looked larger, more ominous, more threatening and much more mysterious.

Ray stood back and looked at his handiwork. A smile came across his face as he read the word he had painted at the foot of the stone work. Next he took the chisel and prised open the yellow paint.

He took this in both hands and threw it over the face of the stone work, the thick yellow paint splattered all over the engraved names and the smooth surface. He threw a second time and the paint ran down onto the ground next to his feet. Stepping back he threw the tin away to the side. He then took the hammer and chisel and moved around to the other side of the stone and looked at the names. He knew what he was looking for. He hadn't been listening to Topham but he remembered the names. He found the first one, Cooper. He took his chisel and put it on the engraved name and hit it with the hammer. He was going to chisel the names out.

He tried and hit the chisel hard several times, smiling. But he stopped when he saw it had not made an impression. He tried again and again, then moved to the other names. Matthews, Peter Summers and Larry Wilson.

No matter how hard he tried, he could not deface the stone. He hit and hit but just could not make an impression or mar the surface. He became agitated, frustrated, and just started to hit the names with the hammer by itself, but still nothing.

He threw the chisel down and stood panting after working so hard for several minutes. He stood back and ducked, startled.

Something had silently flown over him, only inches from his head. He could not see it but he felt it. He looked up but saw nothing. The silence was deafening, even the sound of the crows had gone again.

He backed off, becoming nervous. He looked at the place where he had thrown the yellow paint. His eyes widened and his heart began to beat faster.

The yellow gloss had just run off the stone work as if it was water. The paint had left no stain at all, the memorial was clean, not a mark on it. He shook his head and looked at the red paint he had sprayed on the floor, this was now covered with the yellow paint and you couldn't see what it said.

He was nervous now, frightened. Something here was not right; the night was too still, too quiet. Again something flew above him. He knelt down and looked up.

This time he saw a large crow, the largest he had ever seen, swoop down from a tree. It picked up the chisel in its beak and was gone, flying away with it. He watched as it dropped it outside of the wall, then as it came back and did the same with the hammer.

He wondered how a bird could carry so much weight and still fly, but this big large black crow did. After the hammer, it flew down again and landed on the red paint can he had left on the ground. With powerful talons, it lifted this also and dropped it away on the other side of the wall.

His heart was racing he wanted to get out, he had to get out of this place. He jumped at the sound of a second crow calling from the treetops, then another and another. They swooped down and landed on the memorial. He looked up and saw four of them looking down at him.

Standing, he staggered backwards and slowly began to edge away, but he froze, petrified, when he saw them move. They all took off at the same time and flew in a circle before landing next to him on the bench. He remained still, staring at the vision. Four birds, all looking at him silently.

He shook with fear. He looked at the first, the largest one he had ever seen. The next stood on only one leg, the third was only small, smaller than the others, and the fourth had its head tilted because it only had one eye.

They squawked at him and squawked again. The noise was terrifying. He could not move, he just shook as the watched the birds watching him. He was aware of others but dared not look around, however his fear made him do so. He looked to his side and saw a sight that made him cry tears of fear that ran freely down his face.

Flocks of crows were perched on the trees, looking at him. In the trees, on the ground, everywhere, hundreds of them just looking at him silently.

He looked back at the four on the bench, whimpering and shaking, he was a pathetic wreck. He was scared and he had never experienced fear like this before.

He looked at the two gates, the exit of the grounds, which was full of black guardians looking at him. He turned again and stared at these four main birds. Flashing through his mind was what he had just tried to do, chisel out the names of four soldiers, Wilson a large man, Matthews who lost a leg, Peter Summers a small man, and Larry Wilson who was shot in and lost an eye.

Were these birds here now looking at him the same ones? No. He dismissed it but he couldn't take his eyes off them. They seem to be waiting for something.

Ray eventually spoke, saying, "Sorry."

He was shaking and had closed his eyes. Unable to control himself he urinated down his leg. The fear was too much. He was sobbing and he dropped to his knees. He put his head in his hands and he cried out uncontrollably, saying over and over and louder and louder,

"I'm sorry, I'm sorry, I'm sorry." He didn't know how long he had been there but, when he opened his eyes and managed to stand, he looked around and discovered that the crows had gone.

All except the four on the bench.

One by one they flew away silently up into the trees. The last one to go was the small one, this hopped off the bench and stood in front of him and he looked down at it looking up at him.

It let out a squawk directly towards him and then flew away. He was alone once again. Looking around, he saw the memorial untouched, unmarked. He turned, feeling shaky, scared and ashamed.

Walking quickly, he reached the gate and then ran all the way home. He had an essay to write and not a lot of time to write it in.

The Stranger

She didn't like driving alone, she felt uncomfortable with it, her ex husband told her it was insecurity. He told her a lot of things, mostly insulting and degrading. She had put up with it and tolerated it for many years. But finally, when she found the message on his phone she snapped. She had suspicions before hand but choose to ignore them. But there comes a time when you just can not ignore and bury your head in the sand anymore. He was having an affair and that was the end.

She shook her head and dislodged the thought and the memories that would always follow.

She took a deep breath and looked out into the night ahead, the lights illuminating the way along the quiet road.

She noticed the light come on next to the fuel gauge. Looking at it, she frowned for a moment until to registered what it meant. She felt a surge of panic rise in her stomach and she looked round inside the car, but for what she didn't know. She peered for a moment at her fuel gauge, it had reached the red line, and she was not sure how much fuel she had left. She never let her tank get this empty before, she looked up and back out of her windscreen at the dark road ahead of her.

Unconsciously she slowed down in some attempt to save petrol. She we breathing heavy and a hint of the panic returned. Swallowing because her throat had become dry, she looked was worried and scared. Never a strong person and always a little venerable, she gripped the wheel tight as she desperately looked for some sign that would help her into a town or petrol station.

Always glancing down at the light on her dash board, always following that with a look at her fuel gauge. She didn't know how long she had been driving, but the sign on the side of the road made her smile, then laugh with relief.

"Thank God" she said out load to herself as she pulled off the road following the signs that led her to the small petrol station situated off the main road.

She smiled to herself as she pulled up next to the pump and turned off her engine, very much relieved.

She noticed him walking across in front of her car and into the fuel station shop, glancing round she could see no other cars and wondered where he had come from.

She got out and too a deep welcoming breath of crisp night air, stretching she arched her back and breathed out.

After filling the car to the hilt she screwed the cap back on and closed the small flap to hide it from view, reaching in she got her purse from her bag and went to pay.

He was stood by the door just on the inside and smiled at her as she walked past, she nodded and smiled back. Walking to the desk she paid and turned to leave, he was gone, but she noticed him again out on the forecourt.

Walking to her car, he approached her and smiled a very friendly smile, saying in a equally friendly voice.

"Hello, I am so sorry to bother you but is there any chance you could help me please?"

"I'm not sure and really in a hurry" She said not stopping as she walked to her car.

His face showed discouraging sag and he forced a smile before saying in a disappointing voice.

"Sorry for bothering you"

She walked to her car and looked back to see him still standing and looking lost, her instinct took the better of her and she shouted from her car as she opened the door.

"Are you in some sort of trouble?"

"My wife and child are in the car down the road and we ran out of petrol, I have come here to get some, but they don't have a petrol can would you believe?"

"I do not carry one either, I am sorry" She got back into her car and started the engine. She watched as he walked away and headed off down the road into the darkness, she pulled off slowly and drove out onto the same road.

He looked very nice and he looked very honest, but she could never trust a man again and the hurt and pain was still there.

She caught sight of him in her head lights just as the rain came down. It started slow but with in moments it was steady, she put her wipers on and watched as he curled up with his hands in his pockets and put his head down s he walked.

Not knowing why she found herself pulling up along side of him and taking the window down she shouted across to him.

"How far is it you have to go?"

He stopped and came to the car window, he popped his head half way in and she noticed his big pleasing blue eyes look at her.

"About a mile a suppose maybe a little more, not to far" he said with a charming smile

"I can give you a lift if it is only a mile or two"

Thank you so very much" He smiled and quickly got into the car closing the door after him and giving a little shiver as he sat in the warmth again.

The window went up and she pulled off slowly into the night watching the road and a little worried at what she had done.

"You are a very nice lady thank you, the garage owner was not helpful at all"

"I can not believe they would not lend you a petrol can?"

"Well they say it is not something they do, and were not very nice to be honest"

"So what are you going to do?"

"What do you mean?" he said looking across at her

"About your wife and child"

"My wife?" he said with a frown. She felt a trill of fear run up her spine at his cold words.

"Yes you said your wife and child are in a car up the road?"

"Did I, no, I ate my wife some time ago"

She felt a dread and an empty pit in her stomach as she looked over at him looking at her, his face was serious and didn't look friendly any more.

"What did you say?" she slowed and stopped the car, fear reaching up inside her and making her nervous.

"I ate her in a stew, with carrots and spuds a bit of parsnip, she tasted like pork, they always said it would and they were right, human flesh tastes like pork"

"Get out, Get out now" She shouted at him as confident and as sternly as she could.

He reached into his pocket and pulled out a grenade, he clasped it in his right hand and pulled the pin with his left, with out warning he put his hand under her skirt and rested the cold metal of the grenade against her knickers and crotch.

She gasped with fear and her eyes widened, she tried to say something and rise off the seat away from his hand between her legs, but she could not.

"This as a very short fuse, it will explode long before you can get out of this car, killing us both, I am not afraid of death, It is my friend" he said calmly while looking out of the front window at the rain falling.

"What do you want, please, please, just let me go" she muttered through the tears that were streaming from her eyes and down her face. She could not move and shook uncontrollably.

"Do as you are told, drive and we will have a nice chat." he looked at her and she noticed his eyes had become cold and staring. She shook and just cried with fear and torment, she could do nothing.

"Please, just take that away, please I will… just take it away ….."

"I have dropped the pin, and do not know where it is, now drive along and we will have a chat then you can go home can't you"

"I can't, I can't drive with that there please move it" she pleaded through her tears.

"Fucking drive you whore" he shouted suddenly, making her jump with terror and cry out load with fear.

"Please, " she cried at him

"Drive, Drive or I will blow you to fuck, now get going bitch" he looked at her with a fire of hate in his eyes.

She reluctantly started to dive off but she stalled the car and it halted with a judder, she panicked with anxiety and fear. The whole uncomfortable situation was very straining for her, she was shaking and breathing with broken rhythm.

He stared at her and she turned away, somehow feeling if she didn't look at him the situation would be easier. She managed to start the car and ease it off again driving slowly down the road and crying as she did. His hand moved and she jumped as he repositioned the grenade next to her inner thigh and knickers.

"Do not piss yourself either, I do not want all that over my hand do you understand?"

"Please….." she said but jumped and was quiet as he shouted back at her as soon as she spoke.

"Stop fucking saying that word, Fucking please, please, please" he mocked

"What do you want?" she shouted through her fear.

"To talk to you, for you to drive and stop being a weak pathetic fuck, do you think you can do that?"

"To talk ?" she said not taking her eyes of the road, she dare not look at him and concentrated on driving in the rain and dark.

"They fall for it every time, nice eyes they say, lovely smile they say, charming they say, I am not who they think I am, I am not who anybody thinks I am."

"Where am I driving to?" She tried to calm herself and felt if she kept him talking he was calmer and less volatile.

"What is you name?, you just keep going if you go wrong, I will tell you and you can correct your route, what is your name?"

"Harriet" she said still not looking at him

"I will never know if that is your real name or you are lying to me, I could of course search your bag or purse to make sure but I am not that bothered really to be honest"

He must be unstable and dangerous she thought, he was volatile and she knew nothing of how to handle this situation, but she had a survival instinct and knew she must get somewhere where there were people and lights, someone who could help her, she tried hard to calm herself and drive carefully. Having a grenade in your crotch was not the

most ideal situation to be in, let alone having a mad man holding it with the pin released.
"What does it feel like having a strangers hand on your pussy holding a live grenade, what is going through your head, is it a turn on Harriet?" he asked her serenely.
Breathy heavy and desperately trying to calm her nerves, she attempted to have a conversation with this maniac in her car.
"It feels very threatening and freighting"
"Not kinky then, Not exciting, not a turn on?"
"No, not at all, maybe there is no need for it to be there, I can still drive you anywhere you want to go"
He smiled and then laughed a long laugh out load, his hand shook against her knickers and she flinched and tried to calm herself and drive at the same time.
"Do not even try to play games with me Harriet, or what ever your fucking name is, I have had that many psychotherapists and analysts and doctors talk to me. Did you know most psychotherapist are more fucked in the head then the people they are trying to help, they have these vulnerable and weak people come to them or sent to them, and they just impose there fears and demons onto them and make them believe something that as not even happened or does not exist. Did you know most of them are more troubled, more fucked up, more twisted then their patients?"
"I don't know" she shook her head not knowing what to answer to his question.
"Well it is true, they are all fucking mental, fucked up, twisted evil, psychotic bitches believe me, I fucking know, they should not be let loose on the victims they call patients"
"Where are we going, please just tell me what you want from me?"
"Keep driving and avoid cities and towns I want quiet roads, take me home to your house

we can have a nice cup of tea" he smiled at her and patted her on the knee with his left hand gently.

"I live to far away from here, I don't live anywhere close at all?"

"I could look in your bag and find out if you are lying to me, but I can not be fucking bothered Harriet, or what ever your fucking name is, keep driving and if I see any cities or towns or people I will blow us both to hell, I am a welcome visitor there and know it well, so it is up to you Harriet, or what ever your fucking name is."

"I will try my best to stay clear then" she said in her most claming voice she could muster in this situation she found herself.

"That's better, that is more like it, now where was we? I tell you what, why don't you tell me something about yourself?"

"What like, there is nothing to tell" she said nervously

"Where do you live, what do you like, where have you been, what is your pain tolerance, and what is your most disgusting habit, lots of things"

"I live Near London.." she started but was abruptly stopped as he shouted once again at her with a venomous screech

"NO, no, no, we are a long way from London which is why you have said that, I am not stupid, I am many things but not stupid, it is you who are stupid my dear, now lets start again, what is your most inner fear?"

"I don't know," she shook her head.

"You do, or maybe you don't yet, because if you have not experience true fear you might not really know what you fear the most, so that might be a very good answer. I think you have had family troubles, maybe an abusive father but you just do not realise it. Oh look the rain as stopped" He looked out and up into the dark sky, The wind screen wipers were turned off and she pulled out on to another road, several cars had passed and she had thought of stopping and trying to dash from the car but knew she would never make it in time. Coming to terms as much as she could, with her situation she tried to keep it together and just wait for her chance.

Finding to difficult to drive and getting more and more anxious she tried to ask him to move his hand again.

"I find it hard to drive safely with your hand there, could you please move it, even just a little, please"

"Does it bother you a stranger has his hand on your pussy then" He started to move his hand round and touch her with his fist as he held his grip fast round the grenade a slight malevolent smile came across his face.

Trying not to show her discomfort she edged as far as she could back into her seat.

"It is just difficult to drive, that's all"

"That's all, are you sure that's all?, You might be getting turned on, lots of women fantasise about being raped by a stranger did you know that?"

"I don't know about that but I find it very difficult to concentrate and drive safely"

"Do you now, when I was a child I use to have two rabbits, I kept them in a hutch at the bottom of the garden, one day my dad, who was an alcoholic, decided we would have rabbit for tea, he made me kill them skin them and gut them, he showed me as I did it, my mother was forced to cook them and then we eat them for tea, my two rabbits, which I loved and looked after from little bunnies"

"How old was you?"

"Nine, nine years old, I was always witnessing my father beating, raping, and brutalising my mother, but that was the norm after a while, but the rabbits, well that was just not right I thought. So I never forgave him for that"

There was silence for some time and she drove faster, she didn't know why but she started to drive faster, the rain had stopped and there was more lights along the road, she knew they were coming into more populated areas. Not really knowing what she could do but it caused a slight lift in her attitude and gave her a little hope to cling on too and keep in control. She glanced across and saw the vacant look on his face, he was remembering something and was lost in his thoughts, she felt his hand twitch and feared he would just let go of the grenade as he drifted away with his thoughts.

"So what is your name?" she said in a slightly louder than normal voice to get him back and in control of the grip in his right hand.

"Simon, Simon Pearson, that is my name, with letters after it"

"What do you mean?" she asked curiously

"Never fucking mind, where the fuck are we?" he looked out of the window and noticed houses along the distance and along the way they were heading. His right hand shifted as he swung round in his seat, it was not panic, it was not surprise, she could not put her finger on what it was but he was definitely agitated.

She drove towards the lights, trying her luck she swallowed and bite her teeth together, a glimmer of hope raced through her body and mind.

His hand moved away from her and sighed a little sigh of relief as he was no longer touching her. He peered out of the window and seemed to be looking for something, he shifted in his seat and his right hand moved completely away from her but still had hold of the grenade in it, she looked at him and saw he was facing away from her looking out of the side window. His right hand down by his right knee now away from her, and no longer between her legs. His head up against the window his attention concentrating on something outside.

She slowly moved her hand down and as quietly as she could unfastened her seat belt. it clicked silently as she slowly undid it from its fastening.

She felt her heart beat faster and her breathing getting heavy, he was facing away from her, his hand was gone from her crotch and she was unbuckled from her seat. She looked ahead and saw a row of houses in front of her. She put her foot down and the car sped up, he slowly turned his head and smiled at her. It sent a shiver down her spine but she kept going. Somehow theses houses were her salvation, her escape and she was heading for them. He lifted the grenade up in front his face and kissed it. Then looked back across at her. Before he said calmly.

"Harriet, or what ever your fucking name is, I will always be with you, I will always be in your memory, no one or nothing can ever erase that, so in a way I am immortal."

She opened her door and in a panic and desperate survival drawn action threw herself out and landed on the road, the car veered off and out of control across the road, wasting no more time she got to her feet and ran as fast as she could not looking back.

The houses in front of her were getting larger and larger, she laughed a nervous and broken laugh.

She never even looked back when the explosion erupted inside the car, which had ditched in the side of the road.

The grenade obliterated the vehicle and all that was inside of it, she pounded on the first door she came to and cried and shouted in sheer panic until it was opened, lights were coming on in the other houses as the blast got the attention of the owners, the car was in flames and the street was alive with activity.

It was some time later when she was in the room with a female police officer and inspector that she was told who the man she had given a lift to was.

"He was a well respected psychotherapist for some years, until his wife was found half mutilated and decomposing in his house, he disappeared and must have been on the run for several days" The inspector was telling her, but she didn't listen, she was not even in the room, her thoughts were else where and the memory of the man she had picked up in the rain that night, the nice looking man with a friendly smile and blue eyes, the man who would never leave her memory.

She felt the hand on her arm and looked round, it was the police woman who smiled at her saying.

"We have a councillor, who will help you if you want someone to talk to?"

"No, I don't want to talk to them, I never want to talk to them."

The end

WITCHFINDER

Ray Sibson was hunting her down, he had become an expert and knew how these creatures acted and how they fight. This was not something that he had choose to do, he was an ordinary man trying to live in a new house with a new family some years ago. Until the unspeakable happened there that changed his entire life and existence and set him on the journey he was taking now. But that is another story and another time. Right now he was using his Ouija board, his tool for finding these vile evil things that walked the earth un-noticed by ordinary people, but Ray noticed them and he killed them.
He was sat in his old Ford Sierra, looking at the board, the tool that pointed him in the right direction. then he just seemed to know where they were, he could sense their evil. In the back seat was his faithful friend and companion, Bodie, a large powerful dog. Who had been with him for many years and has joined his master's fight to rid the earth of these devils disciples.
Ray put the board down, reaching down, he checked the hunting knife was in his boot, He looked round the deserted street and down the alley he knew he had to go.
Getting out of the car he opened the back door and let his dog out, who shook himself and looking at his master for the command. Locking the car, Ray, dressed in a combat jacket that hid his powerful build and muscular presence.
Walking, his steady eyes narrowed and the senses of a hawk, he looked round as he walked down the dimly lit alley, Bodie by his side ready to serve, protect, and defend. The night was cool and the rain had stopped, leaving the ground shining with its wetness. The trees on his right covered the railway line, he stopped and looked round, Bodie sniffed the air and the hairs on his back rose and a low growl could be heard coming from

deep in his throat.

"Calm lad, I know" Ray said quietly to his dog in his dulcet Yorkshire tone..

Slowly going down the stone stairs at the end of the alley they both could sense the danger, both knew they were close.

He had learned to trust no one and never take things as they seem, and tonight was no exception. The moon was high and full giving him good light especially now the clouds had disbursed after the rain.

He stopped and looked back into the tress that stretched into the woodland beyond. That is where he must go he glanced round one more time before he went down the steps and headed into the tree line.

Bodie crouched and glared into the black trees, Ray stood silent listening, his heart beating strong but not faster than normal, he was focused and ready. Reaching into the jacket he pulled the large hunting knife he had in a holder under his arm. The one in his boot was always there as a backup.

His breath frosting in the crisp air, he listened to the silence, letting his animalistic sense take over, guide him. It was something he put his utmost trust in. He saw what was in the shadows and heard what was in the darkness, nothing detoured him from what he had to do. Slowly he walked down the wet path and the trees became thicker and denser on both sides. The light was dimming as the trees cut out the shine of the moon.

He gripped his knife tightly and was ready. Like a coiled spring he slowly walked along, ready to launch himself at anything that was thrown at him. He was experienced and he was very quick and strong.

The laugh came from the darkness, a low chuckle, it bolted him into action, two black figures crossed his path, dashing from one side to the other. So there was at least two?. Bodie moved off to the side, he knew what to do and they had an almost telepathic connection. Ray stood solid, he looked an awesome figure, powerful and solid.

The knife came up and sliced through the air in perfect timing as the figure flew at him. It cut and gashed the skin causing the vile creature to scream out an unearthly howl. Blood seeped through the garment it was wearing and it fell in a heap to the ground. The long razor sharp nails dug into the ground as it tried to stand. But Ray was already moving and his boot caught it hard in the face reeling it back. The woman that looked more like a demon rolled back once again in pain. Her eyes red and bloodshot, her skin a dark yellow. Her teeth rotting in the gums, the smell that emanated from her was foul. She rolled away and carried on going, she then was up on her feet with lightning speed, with a screech she dashed forward arms wide and talon like nails pointing forward. Ray dodged to the side and hit out with a powerful fist to the side of this creature, it spun on the spot and unnaturally quick rushed forward again. Ray rolled out of the way as the nails were used like claws and aimed at his head. He took the knife and threw it at the on- coming assailant, it buried deep into the gut and stayed there as blood began to spill from the wound, Ray was moving fast and dodged yet another attempt to gash his head. He kicked out and hit her knee cap, buckling the leg and making the repulsive screaming creature lose balance, he hit out again his fist smashing the head, then face of his attacker.

Again and again he hit it, the cries died as it was knocked unconscious. Ray quickly knelt down and took the knife from his book and with a powerful cut sliced her throat. The blood pumped out and gushed over the floor.

He turned quickly and saw the second witch coming for him, but Bodie had already made her a target, he jumped and with his huge weight and strength brought her down with ease, he went straight for the throat and ripped it with a few shakes of his head. He tore the jugular out and backed off.

The trees began to rustle, something was in them and coming fast. Ray retrieved his knives, cleaned them and put them back into place quickly. He knew the scenario, they had tried it before with him. Offering bait, to try and surround and capture their prey. He quickly dashed off back the way he came, he was falling for it.

Whatever it was, pursued him and his faithful dog it was moving fast and coming strong. But Ray was to cunning to fall for the old trick, he knew he had to get out of there and live to fight another day. He broke into a run and headed back for his car. He bounded back up the stair three at a time and ran through the alley. He was a witch hunter and probably the only one. No one else could do or sense what he could. The skill and gift he had was unique to him.

They reached the car and Ray opened the door letting Bodie in to the back, he looked into the darkness of the trees for a moment, then got back into the car himself. Started the two litre engine up and headed off back down the road.

The full moon shone its power and lit the night sky, the shadows from the trees poured out like a disease into the darkness there was a flock of them, vile, high flying creatures. They all knew who Ray was, every coven knew of him now. He had been hunting and killing them for some time. They had tried many times to trap him, kill him and destroy him, but he was always too clever, too fast and too strong. The car sped on into the night and away, he was ready for anything that came his way. Living a lonely life and existence, travelling the country hunting and killing the evil that lived among us. No one to help him, no one to defend him except his faithful friend, Bodie.

He would be there, no matter what, no matter the danger, he would fight and defend his master to the death.

They never caught him that night, he lives and fights the evil, always ready, always on his guard. The rain turned to snow in the coming weeks and snow crunching under the foot, the breath frosting in the air directly in front of his face, the old farm house was where he was heading. He knew they were there and he had to go and destroy them at all costs…..

The end.. For now………………..

This is an introduction to Ray Sibson, if you want to find out how he became what he is, read …HIDDEN DARKNESS, if you want to follow his quest read the following on books. SISTERS OF DARKNESS, REALMS OF DARKNESS, BACK INTO DARKNESS, SHADOWS OF DARKNESS and DREAMS OF DARKNESS all by the same author,,,, Kev Carter from amazon.co.uk or lulu.com …..

Friend

He was running fast and knew if he didn't keep going, they would catch him, they were always after him and if he can just make it to his own street he will be safe.

His breathing was heavy and he was tired, he ran home like this from school every day, it was no fun and sometimes he felt very ill afterwards.

He was over weight and not very fit, he comfort ate and hated exercise, all this running was not good for him he felt.

"We are going to get you, fatty" He heard them shout with menace from behind him.

He did not look round and just kept going, gasping for air he turned into the alleyway and tried to sprint up along the concrete surface that was under his feet.

Throwing his school bag back with his arm, he was slowing down, he knew one day they would catch him and they would beat him, he knew of an incident where they beat a boy and slashed his face with a knife. A lot of people are scared of them and they are getting worse it was only a matter of time before they seriously hurt or killed someone. He was in no doubt they would enjoy attacking him and would not stop.

He dashed from the alley and struggled up the road, he heard the chants and laughter as his pursuers entered the alleyway from the far side, they were getting closer.

He began to panic and tears filled his eyes, he was crying with fear and just kept going, he knew if he could reach his street he would be safe, they would not touch him there, too many witnesses.

Breathing out with a whimper, and wheezing the air back into his lungs he struggled on. He hated this, he hated being bullied and picked on, he hated the torment of being a victim, he just ran and cried and suffered in silence.

The street was in sight and he headed for the corner, he made it, and didn't look back, he ran up the road and could see his house, he was safe for tonight and relieved once again. He pushed open his small wooden gate and fell to the ground in a heap on the garden. Panting for air and crying. He crawled up and across to the front door, anguished contortions of emotion drove him, he pulled himself up by the handle and fumbled for his key and fell into the house closing the door behind him, he then quickly locked it.

He could hear the voices outside calling him as they went past, he heard the thud on the window as they threw something at it, he didn't dare look, but he felt he was safe now. He cried and sobbed trying to get his breath back, curled up on the floor like a baby.

He stayed there until he had composed himself , he knew his mother would not be home for about a hour so he had time to appease himself and calm down.

He did not tell her because he did not want to burden her, she had a lot of worry on, with her work and he knew she cried herself to sleep some nights, his dad had left with another woman and it had been hard fo the boy and his mother, She had done her best for him and tried to give him what she could, but he understood it was difficult and he had to accept and appreciate what he had and what he was given.

After tea he took the metal bowl and the plastic bottle filled with water, he went out to the small run down shed in the garden and took out the long pole he had there, it was an old mop shaft but it did the trick fine. He also took the bag of leftover food from the dinner table, he always said it was going into the dustbin but he saved it.

Taking these items he walked round the back of his house and down the small path, he dropped and hid behind the wall and secretly peered over it. He had to make sure there was no one in the garden or he was not seen.

He looked across the way and could see his friend tied with a chain and looking beaten, and down trodden, the dog was once a grand animal but now it was a shell, a crushed creature that suffered every day. It made him mad and very sad to see the dog like this and he came down every day to try and help.

He moved quietly and went to the fence, the dog looked at him from the yard it was in but did not yet move, it watched as the bowl was turned and put through the slat of the fence, then placed on the floor, filled with the lef over food from the bag, then the bowl was pushed with the pole to the laying dog.

Looking round he gestured to the animal to eat. With a painful pull on its limbs it struggled to rise and move to the bowl, the chain stopped it going any further. Eating the food it then sat and waited.

The pole was put through the fence and into the bowl, reaching and stretching through the fence he pulled the bowl back.

He took the bottle of water and poured this into the bowl and again pushed it towards the dog, and again the animal gladly lapped it up.

When it had finished he again stretched through and pulled the bowl back with the pole. The boy looked at his friend tearfully, and the dog looked back, it laid back down and just looked at him with patient and sad eyes.

He knew the owner beat the dog and just left it in the yard all day and did not feed it, he had been coming for weeks now and had seen it get worse and worse, he would love to take the dog and look after it, but knew that was impossible.

The owner was a violent and drunken man, he would not have any worry about coming to your house and attacking you, this is what him mum had told him when he wanted him to be reported to the RSPCA.

He was stuck and knew he could do nothing, all he tried to do was get the dog some food and water every day.

He was very saddened to see it, but had to try and help it anyway he could.

He watched his friend as it eventually closed its eyes and went into a tortured sleep.

Leaving he walked home with sadness in his heart he wanted to help more, but did not know what else he could do.

The next day he dashed to school watching and looking round all the way, with a fear and dread he might see the three boys who are after him. He did his school work well, but was always easily distracted if anything happened. He was in constant fear of attack and abuse. It effected his health and his school work. The boys who tortured him with anticipation of pain did not even go to his school. But it did not matter they had shredded his nerves and there was nothing he could do about it.

Most boys welcomed the bell at home time. He saw it as the start of his torture and gauntlet to get home. He saw the bell as a signal he was about to be hunted and tormented.

If they ever caught him they would do him serious injury and would continue to do so, he might even be killed, this was his fear and it eat away at him like a rotting parasite deep within his very soul.

He took a deep scared breath and started his brisk walk up the small hill at the back of the school, through the small gate and across the road, he looked up and down and then across to where he had to go.

Some other school children were walking along which was good, but he knew they turned off on there way before him and he was going to have go the last bit by himself. This was when they chased him. This was his no mans land and his fear grew as he reached it.

It was not long before he was alone once again and he started to run. Up the road and along the path which lead to the open ground he had to cross.

He looked around and could not see anyone but still took deep breaths and dashed as fast as he could, along the uneven ground he had to watch his footing.

His fear grew when he heard the voice shout out across to him from the side.

"Fat boy is here, its about time we gave him a lesson"

He panicked and whimpered a cry as he tried to increase his speed. But this was it, this was as fast as he could go.

The voices grew into a chant, a war cry, as they dashed from the side somewhere, he did not look to see where they actually had come from he just had to run. He just had to get away, to get home and get safe.

"Look at the fat pig run," They hailed abuse at him and his heart raced with fear and the effort he was exerting on it as he dashed forward as fast as his legs would carry him.

His cheeks were red, his chest hurt and his face was streaked with tears, but he kept going. He heard the laughing from behind him as they swore and threw abuse at him, the threats they shouted terrified him, he genuinely feared for his life.

He stumbled and tripped, his body tumbled to the ground and he rolled over in pain holding his twisted ankle.

Crying and shaking he looked up at the three young men looking down at him, they were a bit older then he was probably about sixteen. They sneered and snarled at him as he looked up crying, shaking and horrified.

"We have the little fat pig" One said laughing, they stood round him in a circle, two black and one half cast. He was the one who did the talking.

"We are going to teach you a lesson now, fat pig" he took out a long blade and grinned down at him as he held it up in front of him like some sort of trophy.

All three then started to laugh and then kick at him on the ground. He curled up and held his hands up to protect himself. The kicks hurt and they dug into his body making him cry out in pain and tormented anguish.

"Hay, what the hell you doing" A voice shouted out from the distance.

"Next time we slice you up fat pig" one said and then they ran off over the waste ground. He shook and cried as the man ran up to him, looking down the man pulled him over to see if he was hurt.

"You alright lad, bloody back bastards." The man helped him to his feet and tried to brush him down some what.

"Thank you" he said crying and still shaking.

"You should try changing your way home, if they know you come this way all the time they will just wait for you, diversify lad, diversify, have you far to go?.

"No just over there" he pointed and limped off, he was hurt and in pain, he just wanted to get home to safety. The man watched him go some distance and then went on his way. This time he had been lucky, this time he had been saved, but what about the next time? He limped and lumbered home, crying uncontrollably he went in and cleaned himself up, he washed the marks off his uniform and hoped his mum would not notice.

He was bruised and cut over his body but his face was clean, he had protected that with his hands and arms.

It was Friday and he was at least safe for two days. He was upset and tried to hide it from his mother, he did it well and she went to bed early, exhausted and tired she worked long hours and had a lot of harassment at work, she tried not to let it come home with her but sometimes just could not help it.

He went to feed and water his friend, and had an early night himself that night.

Saturday was wet, rain lashed down and it run down the street like a river, he looked out of the window, knowing the dog would still be out tied up in the yard. He had a pull in his throat as he thought about it, he wanted so much to help it but there was nothing he could do. He willed the rain to stop by closing his eyes. But it still lashed down with a vengeance. It rained all day. And when it finally did stop it was almost dark. He got his things and the bit of food he had managed to scrape together and dashed over as fast as he could to his friend.

He reached the spot and peered over the wall, what he saw made him gulp and shake. The owner of the dog was kicking it, he was drunk and swearing at the poor defenseless animal. Laying into the frail and weak dog, he cursed and hurt it badly.

He wanted to scream out but held his hand over his mouth, he had to just watch powerless as the man savagely kicked and beat the animal.

Finally the man went back into the house. Shaking and crying he looked at the heap on the ground, the dog just lay there shaking, bleeding and in bad shape.

When he dared he crawled over the wall and to the fence, he tried quietly to get the attention of the poor animal but could not. It just shook and stayed where it was. Its eyes staring but seeing nothing.

That night he cried in his bed, he could not close his eyes and could not sleep, he just wanted to go and rescue his friend. Let him out and unleash him, take him home and look after him, he would have a companion and they could go for walks and enjoy each others company. It would be all he wanted in the world right now.

The next day he was up early and sneaked out of the house taking the pole the water and the food he had from the day before. He ran to where his friend was, he got to the wall and looked over, he could not see anything at first, then he saw the chain and followed it with his eyes, to the end, it was empty.

The dog was not there, maybe it had escaped. He looked round to see if he could see it anywhere, maybe it was hurt close by.

He searched but could not find anything, he went to the fence and looked into the yard. What he saw when he was closer made his heart drop with sadness, he cried out in uncontrollable anger and grief . The dog was still there but it had been dumped across the dustbin like an old carcass. It was dead and its head hung down with its tongue hanging out. The sight affected him deeply and he could not look any longer. He hit the fence with his fists and cried out. The dog was dead, beat to death and had, had a horrible life, he could do nothing to save it. He kicked the fence and swore out loud venting his anger. Turning his shoulders hung down his head bowed he cried and cried and walked away. Leaving the pole and water he knew he would not need them again The boy just wandered away, feeling more hurt and sadness and loss then he had ever done before.

Monday morning arrived and he had had no sleep, he was tired, he was upset and he was feeling dejected. His school day went by, he didn't see much of it he was not thinking straight or caring about anything. All he could see in his minds eye was his friend, hung over that bin, dead, beaten and totally destroyed.

The bell eventually went and he headed home, he just didn't care and walked with his hands in his pockets and head bowed, he was in another place and oblivious to his surroundings until the voice rang in his ear.

"Fat Pig time for you to carve up you mother fucker"

He was jolted back into the waking world, he looked round and noticed he was about eight foot from the opening to the alleyway, stood in front of him were the three youths, one holding a knife grinning with a disturbing glee and the other two with hate in their eyes staring at him.

He swallowed and shook in his shoes, this was it, he had no energy to run, they had him trapped, this was going to be it, the end.

He looked at them and could not move, riveted to the spot by trepidation and total fear. Just as they were about to come for him they all suddenly stopped and froze, he did not understand or know what was happening or why they had stopped.

They all looked just behind him and had confusion and fear in their eyes.

He then heard it, it was a low growl coming from behind him, a warning growl and growl of protection and power.

The three youths looked at each other and started to back off, the growl strengthened and he caught sight of something moving out of the corner of his eye, it was coming from behind him and round his left side, it was a dog, a large and powerful dog, the dog he use to feed, the dog he called friend, but now it was in its prime, it was large and powerful like it was before it was beaten and mistreated, it was protective and menacing.

The three youths froze with absolute terror, they looked at each other then they watched

the large animal stare at them and snarl, bare its teeth, the hair was up along its powerful back, it barked and snapped and challenged them all without fear without compromise. They dare not move they were terrified, shaking, they slowly backed off and started looking for a way out, a way to run, one last snap of the powerful jaws shook them into a panic and a mad hasten. They dashed off and away, running like scared rabbits.
The dog came back to his side and they both walked with out worry to the alleyway and out the other side, he was aware of the dog there but he didn't look down. He didn't need to, he knew his friend was there to protect him, and he knew he always would be.
When he turned into the street he sensed the dog was gone, he was alone once again, but now he was wit out worry, he strolled home slowly, something he had not done for many months, he knew they would never bother him again, he knew his friend, his protector would always be there. He smiled and life suddenly looked much better for him.
He got to his door and opened it, looking down the street towards the alleyway and he smiled. He would never be without his friend again…

The End

Kidnap

"It is a perfect plan, you look just like the prick" Danny told his gullible friend, as they drove along in his old car.

"Sod off you cheeky git,"

"You know what I mean, it is an easy way to make fifty grand, bloody hell his old man is fucking loaded and probably has that as petty cash under his bed"

"I don't know, what if we get caught?" Tom said shaking his head with doubt.

"Look I am taking all the risks here, all I need you to do is bloody pose for a photo and probably scream down the phone like that ponce, you do a great impression of the twat now come on its perfect"

"What if he doesn't fall for it?"

"Tom listen to me, I know Callum is heading off for a dirty weekend with that black whore of his, now he doesn't want his family to know so he will go, and tell them nothing. He will not answer his phone because he is a spoiled selfish bastard."

"I don't know Danny, It sounds a bit risky" Tom bite his bottom lip. A look of worry and doubt on his face.

"I heard him talking to the black bitch, he will take her away to a log cabin up north on a lake somewhere, I have already done a signal check with his phone company and signal is very poor up there anyway, so the chances are he will not even be able to get a call from his dad, and I know for a fact he is turning his phone off, he told her this, so they can have a dirty long weekend"

The car swerved as he took a corner to fast and a clunking noise came from the under side of the passengers wheel.

"This fucking car wants condemning" Tom said holding on until Danny regained control and slowed a little in speed.

"All the more reason we have to do this, so I can get my car fixed " he smiled and playfully elbowed his friend in the ribs.

"Fifty grand, do you think that is enough?" Tom said thinking out loud.

"Well I would say he could get hold of that in the time, don't forget we only have about four days until the wanker comes back, we have to get the timing right" he depressed his clutch and had to fight to get the car in gear, it made a grinding noise and finally jumped in, making the car complain"

"Cant find one, grind one" Tom said shaking his head.

"There all in the same box take your pick" Danny laughed.

"It would be safer to walk"

"Are we going for it or what, I think we have nothing to lose but fifty thousand to gain"

"So what do you want me to do?"

"We need two mobile phones that are not traceable to us, so can you pick them up from a car boot or something or buy one from someone who doesn't know you, make sure we have credit on them pay as you go or something"

"Yes I know what you mean I am not totally stupid"

"I will ring him with the instructions, then we will ring him with you screaming, and finally send him a photo of you tied and bound, we will make you look like Callum and then I will go and get the money and we are away Scott free".

"How do you know his dads mobile number?"

"I have my ways, my friend, I lifted it from his phone when he went swimming in the river that time, remember? I told you it was when he and his stuck up friends went skinny dipping"

"How long have you been planning all this?"

"A long time, and now the time is just right, next weekend we have four days to convince his dad we have him, and to give us the money"

He stopped his car and let his friend out to think about what he had said, he knew Tom would come round, he could always persuade him to do anything he wanted.

He drove away and looked in his rear view mirror as Tom slowly ambled into his house, a smile came across Danny's face and he knew his plan would soon be reality.

The day was fine and the sun shone bright from a clear sky, Danny was happy his plan would soon be reality and he would have twenty five thousand pounds to play with. He had this idea last winter, ever since Callum came to the club, Danny never liked him, he always wanted to just smash his face in. Nothing pissed him off more than arrogance and stuck up posh knobs, as he called them.

More money than sense and no respect for anyone, stuck up, everything about this man made him angry, he would enjoy getting the money and enjoy the thought of any repercussions that Callum's Father might inflict on his son.

He had been waiting a long time for a chance like this and nothing was going to stop him, he had the plan and now he had an accomplice to help him, nothing could go wrong and if it did nothing could get traced back to him, perfect plan, perfect day, perfect result. It was all working out and he couldn't wait to get on with it, easy money for a change and added bonus of getting one up on Callum, perfect.

Tom found the phones with ease from a second hand shop, it was one out of town he knew about, the sort of place that would get you anything for the right price and no questions. He had convinced himself about the plan and just maybe it would work. He knew Danny was a joker and a bit of a fantasist at times but he was a trier and a determined one at that.

He impressed him at times, but failed him just as much at times..

Walking with his hands in his pockets he headed down the road, walking steady he turned into Danny's street and saw his friend laid under his car fixing something as usual.

He came up to the side of the car and saw Danny had blocked it up with four bricks and it was lifted precariously to one said while he was laid under it fixing something.

"You are going to kill yourself one of these days, get a bloody trolley jack and some proper car supports." he said leaning down to try and see his friend.

"Bollocks and piss off" Danny's voice bellowed back from under the car.

"Charming" Tom said straitening up again.

"Is that you Tom?"

"Who else is it going to be"

Danny scrambled and slid from under the car, oil on his face and a ratchet spanner in his hand. He stood up and smiled at his friend.

"Have you come round with good news?" he said, a hint of eagerness in his voice

" I have the phones I have credit on them and I have been practicing my most desperate screams" Tom smiled.

"Nice one, we are going to be loaded with in days" He hit his friend on the shoulder and left a dirty oil mark, smiling.

"You are a wanker at times, this shirt was clean on this morning" Tom complained looking down at the oil stain."

"Stop fretting you big tart, you can buy some designer ones soon"

"I don't want designer, I like this one"

"Oh shut up, so you have the phones, right what we need to do now is make sure we can make you look like that prick, I will blind fold you and gag you when we take the picture, so to cover your face some what, I will strip you down as well so to make it look more dramatic"

"No, no we won't strip me down, I am not bloody having that" Tom complained.

"I won't get your dick in shot don't worry, it is not that a good a camera" He smiled and again play punched his friend, leaving yet another oil stain on his shirt.

"For fuck sake" Tom shouted out load.

"Ok I say we ring his dad tomorrow after he has fucked off, I will keep an eye on him and make sure he sets off with that man thing of a woman of his and then we ring, then we ring again and we give him 24 hours, we then ring again with the photo and instructions of where to deliver the money, and then we are rich my friend".

"Just like that?" Tom said looking disgusted at the stain on his shirt.

"Just like that, so stop worrying and give me the phone, it is all coming together and is going to be easy money, what can go wrong?" he said smiling like a Cheshire cat.

"Famous last words, if I have ever heard them"

Tom took the mobile phone from his pocket and handed it to his friend, who took it and placed it in his pocket, with a glee of excitement and enthusiasm.

"Right I am off back home to change, again, and then go over to my mums shall I see you down the pub later or what?" Tom said with a hint of disgust in his voice about his shirt.

"Yes, and don't forget to practice your most terrified scream, I want it full of fear and desperation, anguish and torment".

"Yes mister Hitchcock"

"I want a look of horror on your face, we have to convince him with a scream and a photo so we have to get it right, the only good thing is, he is spoiled twat so they will not take to much convincing, hopefully"

"Hopefully, but I am not stripping off, I can tell you that" Tom told him sternly

"It will be much more dramatic if you are, I will just take a long shot from the side to make it look convincing, you are the same height and look similar anyway, so with the blindfold and gag covering your face it should be good."

"No I am not stripping off, you wouldn't do it"

"Of course I would, I am not bothered I would strip off all day for fifty grand" He said smiling, he knew he would make Tom do it and that is what he was smiling at.

"No, no way, he said shaking his head, right so you are down the pub later then?"

"Be there or be square" Danny said before disappearing back under his car again to carry on what he was doing.

Tom walked off and back the way he came, shaking his head about the stains on his shirt . He liked Danny but sometimes just had to put up with his ways and idiosyncrasies. The thought of fifty thousand pounds was a nice thing to think about and he had already began to think of what he could buy, like a new TV for his old mum, and a few things for himself, he wanted the rest for a deposit on a house.

He thought more of it and the thought of the oil on his shirt faded he smiled and began to walk faster with a bounce in his step, and a smile on his face.

The pub was old and full of character, it was still like the pubs use to be, which is what Danny liked about it, he also knew the place would not keep going much longer it was never as full as it us to be and a lot of the local places had closed. Most of the pubs now sold food and were struggling to get people in.

He sat with his half drank pint, in the same corner he always sat, waiting for Tom to arrive. He looked round and watched a girl over the bar come and collect a few empty glasses from a near by table. She was attractive in a plain sort of way and Danny liked her a lot, but she never paid him any attention or interest.

"You have no chance there you ugly git" Toms voice rang in his ears from the doorway. Looking over Danny lifted his glass up as Tom went to the bar. Minutes later he came over and sat next to him putting his pint down and placing another one next to Danny's glass.

"She is bloody nice" Danny said watching the girl go back round to the other side of the bar and continue with her duties.

"You have not seen her boy friend, six foot six and full of muscles, he is like two men bolted together, and very possessive"

"That's it then, that is why she is miserable"

"He will rip you in half Danny stay clear of her"

"I will take her away for a dirty weekend when we are loaded?"

"What are you going to do with the money, we can not start suddenly slashing it about you know that will just be to bloody obvious, we have to get a story sorted out. There might be an investigation and questions"

"They can not prove a bloody thing, anyway I don't think they will say anything, to bloody proud and stuck up"

"Don't be stupid, of course they will, fifty thousand pounds, is a lot of money, they will want it back when they find out they have been duped"

"Not a lot of money to them is it, they are bloody loaded I told you"

"We still have to be careful so just watch what you are doing"

"This place is going to be gone soon, look there is only four people in here, he looked round and scanned the pub, I remember when you couldn't move in this place at a weekend, full, and stayed full" he shook his head and took a drink of his pint.

"Times change, people can not afford to come out like they use to, it is cheaper to buy the booze in the supermarket and stay in"

"Killing places like this, I have had some good nights in here, picked some talent up as well I can tell you"

"That's it now Danny, you can date on line, you can booze in your home, you have no need to come out anymore"

"Sad and disgusting if you ask me, what as happened to the bloody country where is the back bone and respect gone"

"Like I said times change, people change"

"Makes me sick, I read yesterday there is a bloody footballer who gets over sixty thousand quid a week, all he does is kick a fucking football round a field, they let us down every world cup, they get a kick to the leg and roll on the ground as if they are dieing, makes me sick, what does the soldier on the front line get, less then eighteen thousand a year, he makes us proud every day, gets his arm blown off and carries on. Comes home with no fucking legs and the support he gets is crap, makes me sick".

He takes his pint and finishes it in one gulp, pushing the glass back down across the table and moving the new one Tom bought him in its place.

"Well I can not argue with that my friend" Tom knew Danny would now rear up and get on his orange box and start putting the worlds to rights with his opinions and suggestions. They had many a night like this and as they get more and more drunk louder and more opinionated they become.

"Tell you what else makes me sick as well, this fucking red nose charity day every fucking year, bloody so called celebrities come on the telly asking you for money to send abroad and help Africa, I mean how much money as been pilled into that country over the years, to bloody much."

"It doesn't get to where it is suppose to I don't think, makes a lot of fat cats richer and the poor don't see it all"

Tom said taking a gulp of his beer.

"It would be nice if we had the same for our war heroes past and present, why cant they do one of these things for them? Or the old, who freeze in the winter because they can not afford their gas bills? Or could do with a visit because they are lonely, who helps them out? What about the homeless on the streets in our country?"

"Well we do have poppy day, remembrance day, that is for soldiers isn't it?" Tom added

"Yes but it is no where near enough is it, do all these Wankers come on the TV every year asking for money for them?, No, what happens is some old soldiers or helpers have to stand out side shops and the such with bloody tins, and get ignored most of the time by people, it is bloody disgusting" Danny was angered and his voice had become a few decibels higher, he took another drink and shook his head as he put it down again. The night carried on much the same and they never moved from the place. They went home some hours later and the next day. Tom was sat with Danny looking a little anxious, and took a deep breath.

"Ok try it again, only more desperate this time" Danny told him.

"Why cant we just prerecord the screams ? "

"Because it is much more convincing done live, and it doesn't sound right on tape, you sound like him anyway, just imagine I have your bollocks in a nut cracker and crack one"

Tom squirmed in his seat and screwed his face up at the thought.

"Ok here goes, he let out a scream and it sounded pretty convincing, Danny smiled and said with excitement in his voice.

"Yes, yes that is it, right, when I point to you scream just like that, are you ready?"

"Hold on, hold on a minute, you are sure he as gone and sure this will work?"

"I watched the ponce leave this morning, he will be fucking that ugly thing that went with him by now, so yes the time is right you just scream like that when I point to you"

"Ok lets do it" Tom sighed and wiped his lips with the back of his hand, he could feel the butterflies in his stomach but the excitement was there to and the anticipation of fifty thousand pounds.

He watched Danny as he took one of the mobile phones and punched in the numbers, he lifted it to his ear and waited, then in a disguised voice that sounded like he had bronchitis, he spoke slowly.

"Listen to me I will only say this once, we have your son and if you do exactly what I say you will get him back, if not he will come back to you in small pieces do you understand,

he pointed to Tom and held the phone out towards him, Tom took a deep breath and screamed with fear and panic the best he could. Danny put the phone back to his ear and in his bronchitis voice carried on. If you go to the police, if you try anything stupid, I will send him back to you by post a piece at a time, we have him do as we say or he will suffer like you could never believe. I do not mess about so get this right first time"
Tom tried to hear what was being said but could not quit make out the voice on the other end, Danny had it pushed up against his ear to tight. Something was said and Danny listened, he put his thumb up nodding his head at Tom. Then he pointed and held the phone out again, Tom screamed and in his best impersonation of Callum said "oh god please daddy", he had heard him say this before and knew how he spoke in that pathetic way, calling his parents mommy and daddy even now, he just hoped he sounded right. Danny listened to the phone again before saying in a calm voice.
"I will send you instructions, we want fifty thousand in used notes, and no tricks, or he will be coming back a bit at a time, you have twenty four hours before I ring again, then you get a photo, and tell no one or you will never see him alive again" Danny pressed the off button and then took the back off the phone and the sim card out and gave them to Tom saying as he did.
"Destroy them and get rid of them, we will use the second phone to call the next time"
"So what did he say?" Tom asked anxiously and nervously
"He was quiet at first, don't think he knew what to believe but when you screamed he seemed to jump into life and when you put your little "daddy" touch in there he was caught and hooked"
"Well that is how he speaks isn't it, Daddy, and Mommy?"

"Yeah the fucking ponce that he is, he is getting the money and I will go and get it when I give him the instructions where to leave it, we are going to be fifty thousand better off my good friend" he smiled and punched him on the arm.

Both of them laughed and shouted out loud with excitement and joy.

"It is going to be a long twenty four hours I can tell you that" Tom sighed

"Yeah we will have to get your photo done as well"

"Do it now here, we will have it then, done."

"No, it as to be in a dark dirty place we can not send a photo from here you knob"

"Where then?" Tom asked with a frown on his face.

"I was thinking of that old abandoned mill up on Dalton lane, no one ever goes there and it is cornered off because it is dangerous"

"I am not going into that bloody place it wants demolishing, and to bloody dangerous"

"Exactly that is a perfect place, no one to bother us and no one to see what we are doing, perfect choice, we will get it done quickly"

"No, it is to dangerous in there Danny, the bloody place must be filled with rats"

"Oh stop being a queer, we will go there take the photo and then go and get the money, no one ever goes up there it is perfect, or are you afraid of a little bit of dirt"? he smiled and mocked his friend.

"It is a disgusting dangerous place, you better be careful, what photo are you sending him exactly anyway, and I am not stripping"

"I will gag you blind fold you and tie you to a bean or post send him that, it should be enough to convince him, it will be over in minutes so stop being a big girl"

"Better get it done quickly then, and none of your bloody silly tricks"

"Me?, now would I?" Danny laughed and saw Tom was shaking his head, which made him laugh even more.

Tom was right the next twenty four house passed slowly, he was watching the clock every few minutes to see how far it had gone, he didn't sleep very well and was very nervous.

He was waiting for Danny to arrive and looked out of the window, the sky was overcast and cloudy it had been raining but had stopped now.

The car came round the bend and stopped outside his house he took a deep broken breath and left the house and went outside, he looked up at the sky and saw the dark clouds bearing down on him. He got into the waiting car and looked at Danny who was all smiles and seemed calm.

"I didn't sleep last night" Tom told him as he reached for his seat belt.

"You should of masturbated, that releases sleep hormones you know"

"What?" Tom asked shaking his head.

"It's a known fact, that is why a man rolls over and goes to sleep after sex"

"For fuck sake" Tom looked down in the foot well of the car and saw a rope, and some black long strips of material.

"We will get up there take the photo, then we are almost there my good man"

"Just be quick about it, that's all" Tom was not happy but had agreed to it anyway.

They drove along the deserted road up to the old dilapidated mill, it loomed on the hillside like some large lumbering forgotten monster.

They just did not build them like this anymore, solid stone and all hand done, there was no construction machinery in the day when this was built. It was done by hand and sweat.

The rain started to fall again and began to fall heavy. They stopped outside the large mill and looked up to the many windows in front of them.

"Come on lets get in while we still have light " Danny said grabbing the rope and material from the foot well and he then got out of the car.

They both dashed in and up the stone stairway about half way up and into the building. The light came through the broken windows and from part of the wall that had given way at sometime. Looking round Danny decided on a perfect spot.

"Right just there because the light is coming through the window so we will get a clear shot and I can point it into the place to make it look horrid and uncomfortable"

"It is bloody horrid and uncomfortable" Tom said looking round with a dismayed look on his face.

"Right take your clothes off and I will tie you to that beam there, gag you and blind fold you, take your photo and we can get out of here"

Tom reluctantly started to strip down to his underwear, he wanted it done as quick as possible. It was cold and damp, he shivered as his naked body touched the steel beam that Danny had pointed out.

Danny quickly tied his hands behind his back and round the beam securing them tightly, then he did the same with his feet so he could not move.

"|Hold on, you prat, I can not bloody move" Tom complained as he tried to free himself but could not.

"I want it to look convincing now shut up and lets get it done" Danny said as he took the strip of material and blindfolded his friend, then he took the second piece and gagged him. He looked at Tom and could see he was shivering and could not move.

"Right Tom I am taking the photo now"

There was silence then after a few moments Tom felt the blind fold come off, he shook his head and was relived it was over. He was genuinely scared and wanted to get back dressed and away.

His fear grew as he saw the mischievous look on Danny's face and a wicked smile come across it, he had seen it a dozen times before, just when he was going to pull a practical joke.

"Don't even think about it" he tried to shout but the gag was muffling his voice

"I wont be long Tom I will just go and send this, I do not have a signal here so will go and send it then come back" Danny laughed and thought the joke was so funny.

Tom shook his head and fought at the rope holding him firmly in place, it was not good he was tied and was not going anywhere. Shaking his head he tried to shout and complain but it was no good either because of the gag.

Laughing Danny came over and patted him on the face saying while he laughed

"Won't be long, don't go away"

He left and laughed all the way to his car, he found the joke so funny he could not help himself, he got into the car and looked up at the window where Tom was. He could not see him but knew he would be fuming when he got back, this made him giggle even more, his sense of humour was a not to everyone's liking.

He was not lying about the signal on the phone so would drive until he got one, then send the photo and come back.

He started the car and drove off quickly, the rain was pelting down and the darkness had dropped very quickly, switching on his lights he headed back down the road, the windscreen wipers worked but were not very good the blades were shot and needed replacing. He checked the phone as he drove but still no signal. So carried on some way more. Checking the signal again a little later he noticed two bars in the top left corner, that is enough he looked back out of the windscreen and saw he was not taking the bend in the road fast enough, he hit the breaks and tried to steer round, a clunking sound and a snapping twang could be heard from under the car and he lost control of the steering. He veered off the road and hit the tree with a lot of force it bounced him off and to the side sending the car into a flip, it rolled over and slid down the embankment.

He hit the side of the steel door frame hard and started to lose conciseness, he saw the blood and he felt the pain but then there was blackness.

The light shone into his eyes, he blinked and could not move, he tried to speak but nothing came out, his eyes focused and he could see he was in a white clean room, he tried to turn his head but could not.

"Can you hear me?, can you speak?" The doctor stood directly over him, asked.

"Although Danny could hear him he could not move or say anything, his eyes began to move from side to said, he was paralysed and could not communicate, nothing worked, nothing moved.

"Looks like he is totally paralysed, the doctor said to someone else who Danny could not see, You were in a car accident, you slipped into a coma, can you feel anything can you move your toes or fingers?"

Trying with all his might he could move nothing, feel nothing, say nothing, all he could do was, see and hear, all he could do was listen and watch.

A second doctor leaned into his view and stared into his eyes then said.

"You were in an accident over two week ago, do you remember? you have been in a coma, you have broke your neck......."

Danny heard nothing else all he could think about was his friend Tom..........

The end…

VENTRILOQUIST

The office was not clean, but it was well worked, the place had been decorated a long time ago and from that day on, just touched up occasionally..

The walls had posters and framed programs decorating them, from performers and acts from the stage and screen, most just gone and long forgotten.

He sat there, calm and expressionless, a large suitcase by his side, he was dressed sensibly and tidy, there didn't look nothing special about him, no one would pay him a second look in the street.

That was just how he liked it, he sat on a wooden chair and waited patiently, his right hand resting on the suitcase and looking forward.

He had been there almost an hour now and had no response from the office in front of him. His appointment was for 2.00pm, he had arrived at 1.45pm. The young annoying girl the agent called a secretary had told him to wait and then gone into the office. She was still in there, he had heard giggling and the odd moan. He paid it no attention at this time but it had been locked away in his memory. He looked down at the suitcase and then back at the door.

Another twenty minutes passed before the door opened and a bitchy looking young girl came out, straitening her hair as she did, this was the secretary of sorts who ignored him and walked out the other door. He looked at the agents door which had been left open, he could see inside and an empty desk, a moment later a large over weight man came from the side and sat at this desk, he looked up at caught sight of him, he gestured him to come in as he looked at his watch.

Calmly he stood and took the suitcase in with him, he closed the door behind him and stood in front of this obnoxious man, who looked up and then looked him up and down.

"Ok let me see what you have got, I am a busy man so don't be offended if I send you on your way, what you have to understand is I have seen it all and heard it all, if you have nothing special then you might as well leave now, I have managed the best and know what works and what doesn't." His voice was unfriendly and his body language matched it perfectly. He leaned back in his chair and took a deep breath clasped his hands behind his head and waited, the sweat stains were under his arms and the odour followed.

"Thank you for seeing me, I think I will show you something that you will be very interested in"

"What is your name by the way?" The agent snapped.

"Geoff"

"Do you not have a stage name, bloody Geoff is not going to get you anywhere is it?"

Smiling, Geoff placed the suitcase on the floor and carefully opened it, he pulled out the perfect looking dummy and held it in his right hand as he stood up straight again. He placed his foot on the small wooden chair in front of him and sat the dummy on his knee, he put his hand in the hole in the back and got his hand on the controls ready.

It was a pristine condition ventriloquist dummy, wide eyes, just oversize head but not to much to stand out, dressed in a suite and bright polished shoes, the over all effect looked proficient and professional.

"Let me stop you there before you begin I have seen these acts before and to be honest they are dead as a dodo, drinking water as you say the alphabet, trying to get the audience to concentrate on the doll instead of your mouth movement, it is all old stuff and has seen before, you have to be very skilled and have something new for it to work so you better be good"

Smiling Geoff took a deep breath and looked at the agent straight in the eye, the doll seemed to click into life and the eyes moved round the head turned to inspect the room then it fixed its gaze on the agent, for a moment it just stared at him then the expression changed and the eye brows lifted and the mouth opened.

"Let me introduce myself because it is me you will want not him" the dummy spoke in a very audible voice and there was no muffle or distortion what so ever, just a very sensible but little menacing tone. Geoff's mouth never moved a fraction and he was still and silent as the dummy spoke.

The Dummy smiled at the agent, then the head turned to Geoff who looked back at it and smiled, the dummy smiled back and then looked at the agent once more.

"Get on with the act I am a busy man" He said pulling his hands back onto the desk as he leaned forward.

"Ok, ok lets get on with it, can you please give this man a deck of cards Geoff" The dummy instructed and from no where Geoff produced a deck of cards in his left hand and threw then on the table in front of him.

"Open the pack, see it is a new pack and then shuffle them," the dummy insisted, this was done without any enthusiasm, "Ok now you pick a card, and place it on the table in front of you," this was done as instructed.

"I know you are not yet impressed but just wait and see" The dummy did all the talking and Geoff said nothing. His mouth never twitched, and there was not even movement in his throat, the agent watched and noticed this and knew this man was very good.

"Ok your card was what?" the dummy asked baring its teeth in a macabre smile.

"Three of diamonds" The agent said looking at Geoff and trying to see any movement what so ever in his throat or lips.

"Turn the card over then" The dummy insisted

This was done and it was blank, the agent looked up quickly, he knew it was a trick but had not seen it done at this distance before, he looked at Geoff.

"Magic and a dummy ?"

"Look at the cards please" The dummies voice had become stern and serious.

Flicking through the rest of the deck he was amazed they were all the three of diamonds, he picked at them and rubbed them to see if they were trick cards in anyway, he had just shuffled them and he had just looked at them seeing they were a normal deck.

"Cute trick, is that your best one?"

"Oh no sir we do a song and dance act too, but let me ask you to take something from your pocket and I will show you some magic"

"You need some rapport between you and the dummy, some interaction, banter, you need to speak to each other" The Agent insisted.

"We will come to that later" Geoff said.

"Yes we will. I do not like him speaking when I do" The dummy came back with perfectly.

"I will let him impress you, then we will go into a comedy act as well" Geoff began

"I am the one who impresses you see and then he comes back with some jokes" The dummy carried on to perfection.

"We have many routines, some funny, some amazing, and some that will just leave you for dead" Geoff smiled.

"Right, but before that, take something from your pocket and let me show you some bloody magic" The dummy insisted looking at the Agent intensely.

"What do you want from my pocket?"

"Any fucking thing, just take something out?"

"Calm down and watch your language". Geoff said looking at his dummy.

Reaching into his pocket the agent took out his wallet and placed it on the desk in front of him. He looked up at Geoff and waited.

"Hay, its me who is doing the fucking trick" The dummy spat.

Turning his attention to the dummy the agent stared into its eyes.

"Ok that's good, look at me and I will show you some real magic"

They stared at each other for a moment then the dummy let out a hideous laugh and rocked back and forth on Geoff's knee.

"What?, what is so fucking funny" The agent snapped at Geoff.

"Ok first let me open your wallet, looking down he saw the wallet was opened and spread out on the desk, He looked up at Geoff aghast, sticking out of the inside pocket was a playing card, he took this out and turned it over. It was the three of diamonds.

"Let me close the wallet for you" The dummy laughed and the wallet snapped shut by its self, the agent threw himself back in the chair and the startled look on his face caused the dummy to mockingly laugh at him.

"What the fuck is going on" The agent demanded.

"Well this is just the start, it gets really good in a bit" The dummy said turning its head to Geoff who turned his head and they looked at each other. Then they both looked at the wide eyed and slightly nervous agent who was backing into his chair as far as he could.

"Are you OK?, This is just the start, or is it to much for you?" The dummy asked calmly

"You are not moving your lips, there is nothing there what so ever, that is not a fucking dummy is it" the agent came forward in his chair looking at the dummy in front of him, looking back into his eyes.

"Boo" the dummy shouted and the eyes opened wide and the teeth were bared into a snarl as the face became evil looking for a moment, the agent jumped back in fear but the dummy stayed motionless.

Geoff took the dummy off his knee and placed it on the table laid flat on its back, he undid some Velcro fastening round the arms and pulled these off, he did the same with the legs and the head was pulled out from the neck to revel a wooden ventriloquist dummy, lifeless and in pieces.

He sat down on the chair in front of him and watched the agent carefully prod the wooden dummy on his desk. He picked up a leg and tapped it, seeing it was made of wood, he prodded the chest and felt it was also solid wood.

He was amazed at the skill of this mans Ventriloquist skill, he had no idea how he had done the trick with the wallet but he saw the wallet move by its self he was sure of that.

"You are good, son, I will give you that, very good, but it takes a lot more then just being clever to make it big, you need help and I can give you that help, you were right to come to me" The agent smiled for the first time, but it did not change Geoff's still expression.

"What about me?" the voice came from the dummy on his desk.

"You throw your voice very well I must say you are good at this" The agent said looking at Geoff

"Well it took a lot of understanding to be able to do it, It took me a long time to be able to express it and tame it, and understand it" Geoff said

"What do you mean tame it?, I need you in control, you have to be in control"

"I am in control, perfect control at all times, you are in for a treat and a real show of magic soon. Believe me, something that as never been done before."

"You make me nervous I don't know why, but you do" The agent suddenly put up his guard and looked deep into Geoff's eyes but saw nothing, nothing like emotion at all.

"Well I know you are a busy man and must see a lot of people, I know you have a casting couch and I know you abuse young girls, I know you use people and mercilessly ruin lives, I know much more about you then you can imagine with your narrow, bigoted and selfish pathetic and filthy mind."

Geoff had become freighting to him, he could not look him in the eye anymore and turned away, he tried to stand but could not he fought to get out of his chair but could not move.

"Get out, get the fuck out of my office"

"As you can see, like I said, I am in control and you will now see some real magic."

The agents heart raced, he was petrified, he could not move and he could do nothing about it. Looking at the dummy on his desk he thought he saw movement. He looked again and his eyes widened, the left arm moved, it moved my its self, the fingers stretched out and the whole arm flinched. He stared at Geoff who was looking intensely back at him with a slight, evil smile on his face.

The arm twitched and the hand stretched out and pulled its self across the desk to the second arm, he watched as the arm moved and took hold of the other arm locking it back into place in the torso of the dummy, the second arm reached out and the dummy sat up, pulling the legs back into the joints and locking them into place, the legs and arms were now both locked in and the hands reached down for the head lifting it up and slotting it back into the neck, the head quickly spun round and stared with wide eyes, and mouth open in a snarl, at the agent. Who was paralysed with fear as he witnessed the unbelievable spectacle in front of him. He gulped and swallowed looking back at Geoff.

"My young sister came to you some time ago, she was very talented, a superb singer, nice polite and very naïve, do you remember what you said to her?" Geoff asked him.

"Do you remember her?" The dummy shouted, its head shook in anger as it did so.

"No, no I don't know," The agent could not move he was riveted to his chair with fear and felt the wetness trickle down his leg as he wet himself.

"You said you would do your best for her, you said she would go far, you would take her under your wing, look after her" Geoff continued in a quiet composed voice.

"Please, what do you want?" Shaking he could do nothing, he had never felt such fear or terror running through his bones, the dummy was staring at him and tilting its head to one side as it did, the menacing look it gave him sent him cold.

"She trusted you", Geoff continued, "and you abused her, Cynthia Bothemly is her name, you said you would get her a much better stage name, all she had to do was trust you, she was sixteen, just sixteen"

The face of the agent turned to confusion then his eyes widened as he remembered the girl and how he took advantage of her, he thought she was a run away and took full advantage of it.

The dummy turned its head and looked at Geoff for a moment, then it spun back with a snapping sound to stare at the agent once again.

"You took advantage, you abused and did so much damage you will never know you filthy Bastard, I will be watching you and I will be coming for you" The laugh that followed was something that instantly imprinted its self on his mind and brain.

Geoff stood and picked up the dummy he placed it back into the suitcase, he took the deck of cards from the desk and put these in his pocket. He looked down at the petrified man looking up at him from the chair.

"Don't call us we will be calling on you" He said and with that he turned and left the office.

Silence followed and the shaking was uncontrollable, for a long minute he sat there looking at the door that was closed behind the man who had just left his office. Eventually he shouted out to his secretary.

"Emma, Emma in here now"

Moments later the young girl came in and walked to the desk looking very confused at her boss shaking in the chair with a wet stain on his pants.

"Yes sir?" she asked.

"The man who as just left, with a dummy, suitcase what ever it was, did you see him, did you get his address and name who was he" he spluttered out the questions and waited impatiently for the answers.

"You have had no visitors all afternoon sir,

"You showed the man in girl, what are you talking about, you took his details and made the appointment" he shouted.

"Please sir, I am confused there has been no one here all afternoon, I have not took no booking sir" The girl was genuinely upset and confused and he realise she must have been brain washed or something.

"Oh get out you silly little bitch, get out and stay out"

She rushed from the room crying and bewildered, upset and confused. He looked round and didn't know what to do, he remembered the girl Cynthia Bothemly he remembered taking her to a hotel room, with promises of stardom and important meetings with record producers. He remembered getting her drunk and raping her, he remembered her tears and how it turned him on even more when she fought him off , or at least tried to fight him off. This happened a long time ago and she just disappeared. He put it down to one more notch to his collection and paid it no more notice, he had sick friends who always would give him perfect alibi's and had the security of some powerful people who scratched his back, in return for a supply of young hopefuls who would do anything for the chance of stardom.

He stood up and looked out of the window, searching the street outside, he turned and rubbed his mouth with the back of his hand. Breathing heavy he looked round then left the office, he stormed past the desk where the young girl was still sobbing, he paid her no notice and dashed out of the door. He rushed to his car and got in, he checked the back seat, he looked round like some crazed lunatic, checking every corner, every person he saw. The fear with in him rose and he started the car. He pulled away and headed off down the street, looking in his mirror as he did.

He drove quickly his eyes searching everywhere as he did, he drove home and dashed into his modest house. Locking the door behind him he went into the living room going to the window and looked out of it, up and down the street, across his drive and everywhere he could see. He ran up stairs and got changed out of his clothes. He dashed about, packing a suitcase, just throwing things in. He came down stairs and into the living room, taking a bottle of whiskey from the side board he poured himself a glass, gulping it down straight away, he poured another one.

He went and sat down to try and steady himself a little. Had he just witnessed what he saw? Did he imagine it?, was he dreaming?, the questions flooded into his head as he sat back into his chair and took a deep breath.

He tried to steady himself and then sighed out, he must be safe here, no one could know where he lived. He had friends to stay with until it was over, he knew some people who could sort problems out and they always delivered. Nasty people who ask no questions and break limbs for a living, he would hire a few of these and would not be bothered again, yeah that is it, he would get this sorted out.

The thoughts made him feel better and he relaxed back blowing air out of his lungs and sighing. He sat up and rubbed his face then he saw it, a single card on his coffee table, the three of diamonds.

He froze and started to whimper uncontrollably not taking his eyes off the card on the table. He shook and felt the emptiness in his stomach.

"You see, what you do not realise is, we have been watching you for a long time, we know where you live where you go, your habits your hide outs" it was the voice of the dummy and it was coming from the arm chair behind him.

He dare not look and could not muster the courage to stand.

"Please leave me alone" was all he could say in a weak sacred voice.

"I bet they were her words exactly wasn't they?, Please leave me alone, please stop, please it hurts, please do not hit me, please stop touching, please, please, please"

Geoff walked into the room from where, he didn't see, he looked over to him but didn't move his head only his eyes.

Geoff looked at him with hate in his eyes, standing in front of him he just looked down and stayed motionless.

"What do you want? What can I do to make you go away?" The agent pleaded. Geoff didn't speak it was the Dummy that answered from the chair.

"What you did was disgusting, what you do is vile and degrading you ruin peoples lives and get away with it because you have powerful friends. Well every dummy has its day and today its mine" The laugh that followed chilled his blood and he shook even more.

Geoff went to the side and took the three quarter full bottle of whiskey, he came and put it in front of the agent, he signalled for him to take a drink of it. Nervously he did as he was instructed.

"Drink it all, the whole fucking bottle" Geoff demanded.

"All of it, drink all of it" the voice from the chair added.

"I take it you got Cynthia drunk, I take it you slapped her about a bit too" Geoff said with anger in his voice. With out warning her slapped te agent across the face reeling him back in pain and surprise.

"Hurts doest it?" The voice from the chair shouted out.

"Drink that fucking bottle now, you piece of shit" Geoff said loudly.

The bottle was drunk and he almost made himself sick as he drank it, he gulped and retched a bit, but fear made him do it.

"All of it, drink all of it" The voice screeched from the chair.

He coughed and spluttered but managed it eventually, Geoff took the bottle from him and placed it on the coffee table saying.

"You feel better now do you, more relaxed, a bit more helpless, more vulnerable, less able to resist?"

"More of the drunken, dirty, filthy pig you are" the voice shouted from the chair.

"Have you noticed the rapport we have now, more interaction wouldn't you say" Geoff added. He walked over to the side and took another bottle of whiskey and threw it at his helpless scared victim in front of him.

"Now you get to drink that one as well" The dummy laughed.

Shaking his head the agent tried to plead with Geoff but it was no good the bottle was thrust in front of him and he was made to start to drink it.

"I want that bottle drank as well, because I want you to feel as helpless and as scared as Cynthia did, do you remember what you did to her?"

"Drink, and don't spill a drop" The voice bellowed out from the arm chair in a mockingly way with a giggle and evil snarl.

"I will give you anything you want, money I can get you money" The agent pleaded once more, but nothing he could say would change anything that was obvious to him now.

"Promises, you are so good at making promises, but you don't deliver do you?, you just manipulate and take advantage, you bully and hurt."

"You need to be taught a lesson you see" The voice from the chair rang in his ears.

"Drink the fucking whisky" Geoff shouted and stared with angry eyes at him.

The agent began to take drinks from the bottle, he was feeling sick, ill and he was petrified. The alcohol was taking effect and he could feel his ability to perform being taken from him, his body was not responding to what he wanted it to do. He took another mouthful and dribbled it down his front.

"Time to get the rope I think" The dummy said loudly.

"Rope?" The agent said slurring his speech as he did.

"Yes you must have some in fact I know you do, because you sometimes tie young girls up don't you, go and get the rope from your kitchen cupboard I will wait here, but don't be long.

"Don't keep us waiting now will you" The dummy added

Without knowing why the agent staggered to his feet, Geoff staring at him all the time, wobbling to the kitchen he went to the cupboard and pulled out a rope, he felt sick and dizzy but by some strange force he did as he was commanded.

When he came back into the room, Geoff had the dummy on his knee again and they both looked at him, it was the same pose he had taken in the office earlier.

"Tie a loop in the end of the rope and feed the other end through it, throw that over the wooden beam above you" the dummy commanded.

It was done, swaying on the spot the agent waited.

"Take another drink" Geoff insisted.

As he did he watched the Dummy staring at him with wide eyes and a grin on its face.

"Take a chair and place it under the rope, then stand on it, wrap the rope round your neck tight, then tie it round the rest of the rope so you are secure" The Dummy's voice was mesmerizing and had to be obeyed.

This was done, and the agent was drunk helpless and very unsteady on the chair. The rope was tight round his neck and secured well.

"What you have to realise is, when you hang yourself you have to do it right, a quick snapping action as you reach the bottom of the rope and the neck breaks, but if not, you will hang there and chock to death, it is very unpleasant and painful" The Dummy informed him.

"Please, let me go" The agent managed to say eventually.

"Did Cynthia say them words to you while you raped her, got her so drunk she didn't know what the hell was happening, did you slap her about a bit just for the fun of it" Geoff asked him as he wobbled precariously on the chair.

"He is not looking very well Geoff" The dummy said turning its head to look at Geoff then spinning round back to the agent again.

"My sister never recovered from what you did to her, to shy, to scared to tell anyone she became a shell, empty, a shadow of her bubbly joyful self. You took her life and her dreams from her. Used her for your own gratification and sexual pleasure. Well today she is going to be revenged, today you are going to die and a painful death at that" Geoff told him while he watched him slip and wobble on the chair the rope was tight and felt threatening and he was scared, the whiskey had made him unstable and he began to wet himself again.

"You are fucking disgusting do you know that" The Dummy said shaking its head.

"You've not even said sorry, never asked about her, never shown any remorse or regret, all you have done is offered me money and pleaded for yourself, you selfish bastard" Geoff said as he watched him cry and stagger to one side the rope tighten on his neck. He reached up and tried to untie it, he was desperate and struggled to undo the rope, he lost balance and slipped to one side the chair followed and leaned up on two legs, a cry of terror and fear came from him as his weight shifted and he miss footed the chair completely it fell over and he dropped the rope tight round his neck strangling him, he chocked and reached up, to try and take his weight, but he was to drunk and had no coordination or strength to do so, he began to kick out as his throat burned and the pain tore into his neck, he was gasping for air as the rope chocked him, his whole body swung violently he caught sight of the Dummy laughing at him as he turned round and started to lose conscious. The air supply was cut off he frantically reached and grabbed for the rope but it was no good, he was chocking. His tongue was swelling and filling his mouth, his eyes bulged in their sockets with the pressure.

Geoff watched until he was still, his body turning on the rope round his neck, his body limp, the life chocked from him.

Geoff looked at the Dummy and the Dummy looked at him saying.

"It was to good for him. It should of took longer"

"Well at least, he will not be abusing anyone else will he" Geoff answered

"We should be on the stage you and me, we would bring the house down"

Geoff didn't say anything he walked from the room and then the house, unseen and unnoticed. The body was left hanging there slowly turning and swaying, he looked hideous and smelt terrible, but then again people were always use to him being disgusting.

The End..

EVIL

"There was a fire, but it was caught before any real damage had been done, Mr. Deighton" The estate agent told him over the phone.

"Yes, that is what I was told, so it was not an electrical fault or anything then?"

"I assure you, everything has been checked and has the necessary certification, we can not rent a property without it now, the health and safety regulations are very strict"

"I just want to make sure, you hear these horror stories about places sometimes, I am moving in there with my daughter and want to make sure everything is right, you understand"

"You are covered with our insurance, and in the unlikely event any problems occur, we will send someone round to fix it with in twenty four hours, and if it can not be fixed in that time for any reason it will be made good and you do not pay your rent until it is fixed, no other estate agent round here offers this Mr Deighton, it gives you total piece of mind" His voice was assuring and professional.

Deighton thought for a moment then nodding his head ,agreed with what was being said, the deal was done there and then on the phone, he had to go into the office and sign the agreement and sort out payment details, then the keys would be ready for him to move in. The day was bright and the sun shone high in the sky, he walked with a slight urgency to his daughters school, he was picking her up to take her for her favourite meal, Fish and Chips, she loved to sit in and have a traditional meal with her dad.

They use to do it as a family until the untimely death of her mother two years before of a brain tumour, it was devastating for them both and their lives were ripped apart, they have become closer and more dependent on each other since.

He found it hard to bring his daughter up by himself sometimes, but it was a promise he made to his wife before she died, he would look after her and make sure she was safe at all times. He stopped outside the school gates and looked across the yard, the children had already started to come out, but he knew Sian would not until she could see him arrive. She always waited inside until she could see her dad arrive then she would come out to meet him.

Tall for her age, with short blond hair, pale but healthy complexion, she strolled out with her bag round her shoulder and smiled as she came closer, he smiled back and noticed her mother in her more each day, that child like innocence and natural beauty that was so hard to find in women these days.

"Hi Angel" he said bending down to give her a kiss on the cheek, she returned the kiss and smile and gave him a hug.

"I love you daddy, more and more each day" she said holding him tight

"Love you too princess."

"Oh I am an Angel and a princess today" she smiled and they walked away, she proudly held his hand and felt safe and secure while doing so.

"You want the good news, or do you want the good news?" He said as they walked along.

"Erm, the good news I think, then save the good news until later"

"Ok, we have the house and we move in this weekend, you can finally have your own room and stop sharing with your cousin"

"We have our own place and not have to live with Uncle anymore?" her eyes widened with happy anticipation. Gladness beaming from them.

"Yes we pick the keys up on Friday and can start moving in this weekend, so when we get back you can start to pack your stuff up into boxes ready for the move"

"Fantastic, oh that is brilliant news" she held his hand tight and smiled up at him as they walked along the pavement.

"Thought you would be happy"

"She snores really badly daddy, and I struggle to get to sleep sometimes"

"Well from now on you will have your own room and your own space, I want it kept tidy mind and there will be a lot to do when we move in, a lot to sort out"

"Oh yes I know, and I will love helping you with it, I will keep my room tidy, I do not do mess you know that, so what is the other good news?"

"I bloody love you so much," He said looking down at her as they strolled along.

She smiled up at him and it tugged at his heart strings to see that angelic smile, she had inherited it from her mother.

"I love you too daddy and stop bloody swearing" she laughed and squeezed his hand.

"Well the other good news is that it is furnished so we can just move straight in."

"Oh cool, you are the best" She laughed out with excitement and joy.

They went into the Fish and Chip shop and sat at their normal seat by the window, they liked to people watch, and take the Mickey sometimes, but it was in fun and they had always done it, and knew they would never change.

That night Sian carefully started to pack her things, her cousin was a selfish girl and never offered to help at all, both girls were glad she was moving out at last, it had been a strain staying there, the last few month had been very hard for them all.

Saturday Morning could not come soon enough, Sian was very excited and could not sleep, which was not a good thing because her cousin snored and kept her awake, she always tried to get to sleep before her but it was not easy. Somehow it didn't matter now she was too excited to sleep anyway. She had thoughts how she wanted her room to look and what she wanted in it, this took her mind off the snorting noise coming from her cousin laid in the next bed to her. In a few hours it would be Saturday and they were moving to their new house, alone and with no snoring or cramped living conditions. She was thankful for her Uncle and his wife helping them out like that had, but it was all getting a bit strained now and they had begun to get on each other's nerves.

Saturday morning came and it was time for them to go, her cousin never even said goodbye, their few possessions were put in the back of the car, they had put the rear seats down and just managed to cram it all in, so one journey would do it.

They said there good byes and left, driving away they both looked at each other and sighed out at the same time, then laughed out loud.

"Right lets go and get unpacked and moved in" he said changing gear and heading off up the road.

"You are brilliant daddy, and I know we are going to be very happy here in our new home, with no snoring" she said laughing.

"And decent cooking"

"Oh yes, auntie's culinary skills did leave a lot to be desired I must say"

"Well it was nice for them to put us up, so I suppose we shouldn't complain", he paused and thought for a moment, "but her cooking was bloody bad"

They both burst out laughing and could not help themselves.

"Sometimes I dare not ask what the hell it was" Sian said as she laughed uncontrollably

"Better we didn't know I think, that woman burnt everything, so it all just looked the same and tasted of a charred sacrifice ….. Well actually I don't know what it tasted like"

"Undomesticated I think the word is, I wonder what your brother married her for sometimes, don't you?"

"Well it wasn't for her cooking that is for sure"

They both grinned and felt good, it was going to be a fresh start and something they both needed, it had not been an easy time after the death of his wife. They needed this house as a building block and new way of life.

He pulled up outside the modest two bedroom detached house and stopped, he looked up at the stone-cladding which ran across the building and waited for the reaction of Sian.

She looked at the house then up and down the road, she turned and smiled at him saying "I love it, it looks really nice dad" She got out of the car and stood staring up at the house that was to be her home from now on.

He got out and locked his car, he walked on and up to the house, followed by his eager daughter, excitement in her eyes, and a bounce in her step.

Turning he looked down at her, as he put the key into lock.

"Are you ready?" He asked

She nodded and was eager to explore the inside. He opened the door and they both walked in. It was a welcoming house, clean and tidy, the place was modestly furnished and looked homely. They both stood looking round the room, the wooden banister that lead to the upstairs, the door to the right which was the kitchen, the marble effect fireplace to the left. Windows looking out to a small garden on the back wall.

Sian looked round and got a feel for the place, she closed her eyes and just stood there for a moment, listening and feeling the atmosphere. Deighton walked past her and into the kitchen, he had been earlier and got some essentials like milk and tea bags, at least they could have a cuppa now they were here.

"Going up stairs daddy" he heard his daughter shout, then the sound of feet running up the wooden stair case. He left her to find her way and explore the house for herself, he made some tea and looked out of the back window into the small garden. His thoughts drifted to his late wife. The way she use to tend to their garden, the way she use to love planting things and nurture then to grow.

After looking at the toilet, and main bed room at the front of the house, Sian looked into the airing cupboard and across the small landing, her excitement showed on her face, she liked this house and the freedom it would give her away from her cousin and uncle. She finally ended up in the back bed room, this was going to be her room. She imagined, with it being the smallest. A single bed and small set of draws beside it, a wardrobe stood unobtrusively in the corner. Some shelving and a small radiator on the far wall. The curtains were open so she walked to the window. Looking out across the garden to the house across the way, she scanned the area and smiled to herself. Turning she looked round the room, it was her space, her room, the far wall was bare, it looked empty and cold, but she would soon change that. She already had ideas to where she was going to put things and the lay out she was going to have, the posters she wanted up on the walls and the small lamp she wanted by her bed side.

"Sian, teas up" She heard her dad shout from down stairs a few minutes later, she skipped out of her new room and down the stairs. The room was empty, silent, the door was ajar, but slowly it began to open steadily and rocked open wide, before stopping abruptly.

After they had had their tea, they began to unpack the car, moving all their things in and putting things away, they both knew what they had to do and just got on with it. Clean bedding was put on the beds, things stacked away in the kitchen, Clothes put in wardrobes, and personal belongings found new places to sit.

It was busy but they both enjoyed it. As Deighton was putting some clothes away he looked out of the bed room window and saw a small elderly woman. Stood on the other side of the road looking up to the house, she noticed Deighton and just stared at him blankly. She had sadness in her eyes, and a lived in face, emotionless, she stared for a few moments then took her gaze away as she moved on up the road not looking back. Deighton watched her go, he thought she must be in her seventies, then paid her no more attention and carried on with what he was doing.

The day went quickly and they got a lot done, both were tired but had enjoyed their tasks, and it was all the more fulfilling doing it together.

Before they knew it the darkness had fallen and it was mid evening. They had been working all day and eaten in between. Deciding to go to bed they turned out all the lights locked the door and headed off up the stairs. Sian brushed her teeth and went into her room, closing the door behind her shouting a good night as she did.

Deighton washed his hands and face and brushed his teeth, he looked at himself in the mirror, deep into his own eyes, he missed his wife and the companionship he had with her. The special bond you have when you find your soul mate. That time you find your perfect partner. The most important thing in his life now was his daughter. He wanted to give her the best he could and would make sure nothing or no one stood in his way, or her happiness.

Their first night was uneventful, they were both more tired than they realised and fell to sleep almost instantly.

Sian woke the next morning and opened her eyes, she rubbed them and waited for that few moments, for them to focus. She looked round her room and smiled, her very own space, her very own world.

She stretched out and yawned, then lifted her body to sit on the edge of the bed, she had a small tee shirt on and nothing else. She looked round the room then suddenly felt strange. She frowned and looked round to every corner, she was alone but felt as if someone was watching her, staring, she could feel their eyes looking at her. She folded her arms and hugged herself, shaking it off she stood and got dressed.

He father was already up and cooking some bacon, she smiled and her eyes widened at the smell as she came down the stairs.

"Good morning wonderful father" she said going to the fridge to get some orange juice.

"Good morning wonderful daughter, I thought the smell of bacon would bring you down"

"Oh you know me so well" she said smiling and sitting at the table.

"Did you sleep well ? he asked as he made a bacon sandwich for her and brought it over on a small plate.

"Like a log, and you?"

"Like a log" he smiled and watched her face light up as she bit into the sandwich. He knew how to make it for her just the way she liked it, plenty of bacon some brown sauce and cut diagonally not squarely. He went to get his own and he joined her at the table.

After their breakfast, Sian insisted on washing up, and then she went back up to her room. On entering it she instantly smelt the cigar smoke, but could see nothing. She curled her noise up in disagreement at the smell, walking to the window she opened it and thought it might be coming from outside. But the day was fresh and bright, no foul smell out there, she turned back into her room and noticed the smell was subsiding, she looked round and had no idea where it could have come from. She froze for a moment when she saw her t-shirt she had been wearing was gone, she knew she had put it on the bed, she always did for the following night. It was not where she left it, she looked under the bed and all round but could not find it. Panic began to rise and she shouted for her father.

He came running up the stairs and into the room, worried and confused at her cry.

"What is it darling, are you OK?" He said looking round the room.

"Something is wrong" she said shaking her head and wondering if she had over reacted.

"What, what as happened?" he came to her and she grabbed his arm.

"My Tee shirt is missing, I put it there on the bed before I came down and now it is gone, and I smelt a strange smell when I came up to my room like a horrid cigar smell"

Deighton looked round, he could see or smell nothing. But could tell his daughter was distraught somewhat.

"It probably came from outside darling, someone walking past or something?" He knew it was not convincing but he nothing else to explain it, he walked and looked over her bed and then under it, there was no sign on the Tee shirt. She sighed and smiled, she had calmed and felt a little foolish. The sight of her father there with her, made her feel better, safer and happier.

"It will turn up I expect, sorry dad"

"Hey you have nothing to be sorry about, it is a strange house and we have to settle in

and feel comfortable here so do not worry" she hugged him for a long time and then smiled as he left to go back down stairs, she carried on with her room, opening the window to let the sunday air in, she carried on rearranging and sorting her clothes out. Deighton was stood in the front room looking out of the window a short time later, he again saw the woman he had seen the day before, she was stood looking at the house again. He moved and went to the front door, he made the excuse he was going to his car and when he reached it he made the point of looking at her and saying with a smile.
"Hello"
She looked at him, worry in her eyes, and pain on her face.
"Hello", she said slowly
"I noticed you looking at the house yesterday, and today you are here again, is everything alright?"
"No, you should not have brought your daughter here, no child should ever live in this house again, it should be demolished"
"I beg your pardon?" Deighton said a little unprepared for her answer.
"If you love your daughter, leave this place and never bring her back to it" She looked at him with sadness in her eyes and with an urgency in her voice.
"Look I do not know who the hell you are but don't start with this kind of crap to me, you won't scare me off and you will be sorry if you try what the hell are you saying and who the hell are you anyway?" Deighton said angrily.
"I live at the end of the next street in a bungalow, you can not miss it, all the neighbours call me a witch and an old hag, but they have no idea, I know what went on in this house and you are going to have to get your daughter out and safe because if you don't....."

She was not allowed to finish before he forcefully butted in on her.

"Right listen to me, I do not know who you are and I do not care, I'm an easy going bloke, but don't you ever come here to my house again, don't you ever speak to my daughter, It will be a fucking sorry day for you if you try." Deighton frothed with anger and stared at this woman in front of him. She said nothing and just shook her head, she slowly turned and walked away her head bowed and her fragile frame being carried on not too strong or stable legs. He watched and as his anger subsided, he felt sorry and regretted swearing at her. She did not look back and he watched her turn the corner at the end of the street and was gone. He sighed and looked round the place, it was a sunday and quiet, not many people about and nothing strange, he looked up at the house and thought for a moment about what she had said. He dismissed it and went back in.

It was late almost midnight when he heard the screams, he bolted up in his bed, startled and not sure if it was a dream, he listened breathing heavily, his eyes widened with fear as he heard the terrified scream of a young girl, and a raspy deep laugh from a man, he dashed from his room and bolted to Sian's room, he burst in and looked at his daughter. She was fast asleep and calm, the room was empty and still, the screaming had stopped and he looked round frantically.

It was still and silent, he looked at his daughter quietly sleeping in her bed, the window slightly open and the curtains gently moving in the night breeze, he sniffed and smelt the cigar. He looked round once again and saw nothing.

Walking to the window he looked out into the street, it was empty and quiet, he turned back into the room and the smell had gone.

Taking another look round he quietly left the room and went back to his bed. Putting it down to a bad dream he laid there, but was unable to get back to sleep, he listened for the rest of the night and even went to check on Sian a few more times before she got up. He said nothing to her about what had happened and she was none the wiser.

Her school day went good, her father picked her up from the gates, they drove home in a happy mood, He said nothing to her and hid his concerns well.

They bothered entered the house and settled down for a much wanted cup of tea before going to get changed, Deighton listened as Sian went to her room, she was quiet in there and came back out a few minutes later changed and smiling.

He was relieved, and just went up himself for a shower, he smiled and shook his head, it must have just been a bad dream, his mind playing tricks on him, he felt a little foolish at thinking it could be anything else. He was tired from being up most of the night and enjoyed his shower, it seemed to revitalize him and make him feel much better.

Sian read a book while Deighton did a little work he had brought home, the night went quickly and they both had an early night.

Deighton laid in bed and listened he had left his door open, he could hear nothing and his daughter was safe in her room, nothing was in there, he had checked, the ranting of an old woman was not going to bother him. The smell just came from outside, it must of done. She just misplaced her tee shirt, it will turn up. A new house, strange place his mind plays tricks on him, hearing things, smelling things, he smiled at the absurdity of it. Turning over he pulled the covers over him and closed his eyes.

The night was still and the house was quiet, both Sian and her Father were asleep. Neither of them heard the low toned laugh, the smell of the cigar, Sian was unaware of the sheets being slowly pulled from her body as she laid asleep. Her young body sprawled out and her Tee shirt lifted high. The shadowy figure stood above her, the foul smell coming from his breath, the cigar gripped in his teeth, the old dirty clothes he was wearing. The lust in his eyes as he looked at her young body. He began to chew on the cigar, covetousness on his face looking at her laid there below him. An evil growl emanated from his throat. His eyes widened as he stared at her.

Sian woke the next morning, chilly with no covers on her, she crawled out of bed and rubbed her face, got dressed and paid nothing in her room any notice. If she had looked more closely she would have noticed her clothes had been searched through and her drawer slightly opened where she kept her underwear.

She went to school totally unaware she had been looked at most of the night in her bed. Deighton dropped her off at school and came back home he was taking the day off that was owed to him, he drove back and came round the corner to see the old woman once again on the pavement looking at the house.

He stopped the car and got out walking up to her he was about to speak but she spoke first saying positively.

"He is back, the cigar chewing bastard is back, and he is after your daughter"

Deighton looked at her as she stared at him, she could see the doubt in his eyes and knew something was wrong.

"Who are you talking about?" he finally asked.

"He was a paedophile who took children to this house, raped and mutilated them, just one got away and she was able to tell her father, he came down here and killed the filthy bastard, in the rage and fight that followed, but he returns and must be burnt out and destroyed, this house must be destroyed"

"I want to talk with you, will you come in" Deighton found himself asking calmly, which surprised him but he seemed to have no control over it.

"No, I do not want to go into that house again, you must leave and get your daughter to leave with you" she was very insistent and pleaded almost with him.

"Where can I find out about the history of this house, who lived here?"

"I have told you, he was an evil man, a murderer and child killer, has something happened, what has happened?" She pulled his arm and looked deep into his eyes.

"Nothing, nothing has happened" Deighton told her pulling away from her grip.

"You are lying, he is back and he will take your girl, get her out of here, are you stupid, are you that stupid, you can not see what he will do."

"Who? what will who do, no one is living here except me and my daughter"

"He has always lived here, he was born here, abused by his father, disowned? by his mother. You are not alone in that house, he needs to be burnt out, the house needs to be destroyed"

Deighton did not know what to say or do, he didn't want to believe this woman but could not help being pulled in by what she was saying.

They spoke for another twenty minutes, she just kept repeating herself and eventually they parted none moving ground or getting any further.

He searched the house from top to bottom, he searched Sian's room three times and found nothing, no one was in that house except him, the doors were locked and bolted from the inside, even if they had a key they could not get in.

The words from the old woman rang in his ears, he looked on the internet and tried to find some information on the house but found nothing. There was not a library close by so he could not check there, the estate agents were no help either. All he had was the ranting of an old lady. He tried to dismiss it but could not. Again he went up to Sian's room and sat on her bed, the room was tidy and clean, nothing strange about it at all. He sighed and went back down stairs, he waited for his daughter to come home and took her out for dinner. It was a nice treat for her and they had a good time together. It was half past nine when she went to bed, he watched her go up and listened while she brushed her teeth, then go into her room, all was silent and he locked up the house, all the doors were locked and bolted from the inside. All the windows were secure, no one was getting into this house without him knowing about it.

He fell into a restless sleep that night but it didn't last long, the scream of his daughter and the evil growl that turned into a laugh woke him, like a bolt of electricity. He dashed into Sian's room. It was empty, the window firmly shut, the house was secure.

"Sian, Sian", he shouted and frantically searched the room and house, Running round distraught and fear ridden he could not find his daughter, but he could hear the deep laugh, where it was coming from he had no idea.

In an anxious bid he ran from the house and down the street, not knowing what was driving him to do it, but he turned into the next street and looked for the bungalow, he saw it and ran towards it, just hoping it was the right one.

Banging on the door he screamed out for them to open, a light came on and the window opened and a voice from behind the curtain spoke.

"Go away leave me alone" The voice was weary and full of pain.

"He has Sian, he has my daughter" Deighton screamed.

Moments later the old lady opened the door and came out, she was in a dressing gown and she grabbed him by the arms, saying to him urgently

"There is a door in the wall in the back bed room, it is covered up now, it goes up into the rafters, where there used to be another room, she will be there, that is where he use to hide the bodies, you must be quick, go, go and kick the wall in"

Without a moment's hesitation he ran off back to his house, the old lady went back into her bungalow, only to reappear moments later with an over coat over her dressing gown, she hurried up the street and followed him round the corner.

Deighton was breathing heavy he blindly ran back into his house, up the stairs and into the back bed room, Sian's room, he looked at the wall and kicked at it, nothing seemed to give he banged it and kicked it then he heard the hollow sound, it was a false wall. This was it he kicked and punched the wall, it soon broke. The wooden door that had been disguised behind the ply wood was there. The laugh echoed in his ears, the evil annoyed shout coming from somewhere, but he didn't know where stifled the air round him.

He ripped and kicked at the wooden wall and pulled the ply wood free and off, he was faced with a door, he pulled it and hit it but it was locked. He looked round in a frantic search for something, anything to get him into that locked door.

He froze when he saw the old lady, stood there in the doorway, she held up her hand and he saw she had a key in it. Without saying a word, he took the key from her and was not surprised when it fit the door, he opened it and peered in, he saw his daughter looking up at him from the small compartment, how she got there he was not concerned at this time he reached down and took her out reached arm, she had a gag round her mouth and was crying, scared and shaking but she was alright. He pulled her up and brought her to him, taking off the gag, she hugged him and cried.

The cry of anger filled their ears and the room shook with the noise of this vile man who use to live here. Looking at the old lady, Deighton asked.

"How the hell did you know?"

"That is where he put me when I was only six, but I got out and locked the door, I ran and told my father, I have kept the key ever since, Take your daughter and leave this house, don't ever return to it"

He read later that the house had been burned to the ground some weeks later, but he never told anyone about the old lady, and he never told anyone what had happened. All he knew was his daughter was safe, and he would never doubt the ranting of a little old lady again.

The End…

Printed in the USA
CPSIA information can be obtained
at www.ICGtesting.com
LVHW041547231024
794631LV00009B/64

9 781291 479218